Luna

Luna

JULIANNE BIGLER

Published by Julianne Bigler

Publisher's Cataloging-in-Publication

Names: Bigler, Julianne, author.
Title: Luna / Julianne Bigler.
Description: First edition. | [San Diego, CA] : [Julianne Bigler], [2022] | Includes bibliographical references.
Identifiers: ISBN: 9780578355641
Subjects: CSH: Rabbits--Fiction. | Parapsychology--Fiction. | Quests (Expeditions)--Fiction. | Travelers --Fiction. | Self-perception--Fiction. | Self-realization--Fiction. | Desire--Fiction. | Self- actualization (Psychology)--Fiction. | Spirituality--Fiction. | Belonging (Social psychology) --Fiction. | Social integration--Fiction. | Self-evaluation--Fiction. | Existentialism-- Fiction. | Self-esteem--Fiction. | LCGFT: Animal fiction. | Fantasy fiction.
Classification: LCC: PS3602.I3665 L86 2022 | DDC: 813/.6--dc23

ISBN 978-0-578-35564-1

Illustrations: Charles Lister
Design: Hannah RMS

First Edition

A prayer.
For myself.
For you.
May you be found,
whole.

It's here in all the pieces of my shame
That now I find myself again.
I yearn to belong to something, to be contained
in an all-embracing mind that sees me
as a single thing.
I yearn to be held
in the great hands of your heart—
oh let them take me now.
Into them I place these fragments, my life,
and you, God—spend them however you want.

Rainier Maria Rilke

_L_una lived in a humble home made of clay with a thatched roof along a dirt road. This abode stood in a forest of poplars, wild grass, and blackberry bushes. The woods mothered every kind of furry and feathered creature that lived there. She drove them to their beds in winter and beckoned them to fields of grass on summer evenings. She watered them with droplets plopping from leaves' hands catching the rain. She fed them berries and apples and skies filled with orange cream. Like a good mother, she washed her saplings till their fingers sparkled chartreuse in the sun. She embraced them on sultry summer nights where the warmth of her breath told them they were immortal. At night she rocked them to sleep in a whispered breeze, a distant howl or the silent roar of stars burning. It was a type of sublime we call ordinary.

Luna spent her days in these woods out by the pond near her house, studying at her desk, or caring for her vegetable garden, if the season called for it.

Sometimes, if she had just gotten home from a walk in the woods or around the pond, she would hastily pack a basket with several tidbits to eat and rush to the home of her friends, Chestnut or Hickory, whomever she most wanted to share what she had seen or pondered that day.

Other times, especially in the spring when the morning sun came streaming through her bedroom window, she awoke with a sense of urgency, feeling that she must go see Hickory or Chestnut right away to tell them how glorious the sun was, or how dark the night had been—and that it wasn't anymore. The urgency may have been brought about (without even Luna herself knowing) by some dream she had had the night before. At times she dreamed that she had fallen down an abyss and woke up with a start in the stillness of her bed, fur matted with sweat.

Although she felt flooded with relief, an uncanny feeling of spaciousness followed: a drowning in space she could never use. A mysterious distance lay between herself and what she needed to be real. With restless legs, she would rise and span a portion of the space, not knowing what she was looking for. Walking absentmindedly to her fireplace, bookshelf or desk, she tried to fill the space that surrounded her, or touch enough things in hopes that she might find what she was seeking beyond her own body. While filling these spaces in postures made sense during the daytime, in the darkness they were only soporific, mechanical actions. *This is how one sits in a chair ... this is how one looks out a window.*

Attempting to employ the time by doing a useful activity didn't fill the space; it was usually abandoned shortly after beginning. All productive activities seemed alien and nonsensical in the stupors of those obscure hours. Some final attempts left her to go outside and lie supine in the clearing just down the path from her home, if it was warm enough. The stars seemed to be the only remedy that could dispel the space. It felt less apparent, almost irrelevant compared to them. She might think of her friend Hickory, the otter, and wonder if he were sleeping the night through.

Dawn was the end hoped for, and the night a necessary penance endured, as though the space would be swallowed up with the passage of time—an allotted amount of ticks from the clock or breaths taken— when the sun declared this vacuous time at an end.

She felt as if this excess of space lasted, as nights tend to do, for an eternity. And she would finally give in to sleep as the stars began to fade in the smoky blue of dawn.

Autumn crept in through the tips of the trees. The red maples, the oaks, and the sweetgums redecorated, subtly, as though modesty made them reluctant to flaunt their elegance. The air grew damp, wind leapt from the leaves, and Luna felt she should change. The forest itself morphed into its new season as though packing up for a trip. *Where does it go?* Luna asked herself. *And why do I feel left behind?* It was unthinkable to stay the same while the world was changing before one's eyes. An isolation spawned inside her, one that drew her to take long walks or visit Chestnut's home in a tree.

A flock of geese flying past her window seemed to diminish the size of her home, in which she quickly felt cramped, with the promise of something happening elsewhere. She felt the sheer mystery of where they were flying gnawing at her.

She packed her bag without planning on going anywhere in particular. Snapped and ready, it sat by the front door; not as a convenience, but like a hole dug that had not been filled.

Luna made short excursions, ones that didn't require the conspicuously neglected bag by the door. During one of these autumnal trips, she made a puzzling and not slightly disturbing discovery.

She had gone for a walk along the yellow cottonwood trees that skirted the pond near her home.

Feeling more aware of the millions of cordate leaves quivering in the wind than her own body, she almost managed to make it home without having breathed at all, that she could remember.

Just as she reached her yard, she paused and looked behind her, staring at the path she had taken home. A layer of fine dust lay on top of the dirt road, which had the imprints of Chestnut's raccoon paws from her previous visit, a hedgehog and her four children, and a quail with her five progeny perpendicular to the path. Even a snake's wave undulated across the sand. But she noticed something missing: where were hers?

I just walked there, she thought. *And Chestnut hasn't walked this road since yesterday.*

Feeling uneasy, she turned and continued. Dusting off her feet on the bamboo mat at her front door, she didn't look back at the road. Taking her garden hose, she took extra measures to clean her feet before going inside. *I do not want to track in any loose dust or get dirty paw prints on my floor,* she told herself, willing the occurrence out of her mind.

The next day a cool October rain fell. Luna wanted to go to the pond and watch the rain fall on the water. She liked to watch the surface and imagine the sound of millions of raindrops under water.

She put on her rain boots, coat and hat, and set out for the pond down the road.

On her return, her boots sank into the mud, causing a sucking noise with each step that made a rhythm to her stride. The rhythm broke when one foot came out of her sunken boot. As she turned to pull the boot out of the mud, she noticed the road behind her. She was stunned. Beyond her last three footsteps, the muddy road was completely smooth. She stared at the path behind her, her bare foot still in midair. How could there be no footprints behind her? A chill came over her and her fur bristled. Her heart began to race. Hopping awkwardly on one foot, she shoved her other foot back into the boot and leapt toward home.

AUTUMN FADED AS snowflakes fell. Nothing is more dependable than seasons changing. Change stays the same. But amid the change, there was no continuity. Luna wanted to change with the forest as a horse spins along with its carousel. Yet her change was disjointed, her own seasons poorly sewn together piecemeal. Fragments of the forest blew away—leaves, flocks of birds, dandelion seeds—and she wondered where they were going. Every year the forest told its story, a prodigious wheel that revolved over and over again. What was she—a scrap that had fallen out of a painting, now with a life of its own? A loose cog in a clock? She watched from her residence in the woods like a detached yet anxious observer.

She did not speak of the strange occurrences that had happened the previous season. The very thought of them was fearful.

The seasons blew in and out. Blossoms blew off tree branches and Luna's footprints were nowhere to be found. She wandered through tall grasses and left no path. She shuffled through sheets of orange leaves that rustled back to their places again. She spoke of it to no one. Only she spent hours underneath the trees or in front of a fire with Chestnut and Hickory with a breathless uneasiness. What good was any of it if it didn't last or build upon itself? What belonged to her? The little blossom cyclones swept up by the wind, the peach trees, the patches of sunlight over her face, none of it. Chestnut and Hickory? No. That was the worst of all. They were not hers, and she was aware of it even in their joyous times together.

ONE WINTER NIGHT Luna was visiting Chestnut. They had spent the cold day walking around the frozen pond, then prepared bread and stew for dinner. It had snowed for several hours but had stopped sometime after dinner. Outside, a dim blanket of snow lay in the dark.

They reclined near the fireplace after their meal, Luna with a book and Chestnut a tablecloth she was embroidering. A tabletop clock rested on a side table next to them. Its second hand was loud and alarming, and Luna felt each tick as though it were a stick tapping her shoulder. It seemed to be ticking down to an end rather than traveling around an endless circle. The sound was harsh and offensive, though she had never noticed it much before. It was just past nine o'clock.

"Are you sure something isn't bothering you?" Chestnut asked, her eyes on her needle.

"Bothering me?" Luna repeated nonchalantly while she steadied her breathing.

"You seem distant or nervous. You were the same at the pond, too. Am I just imagining it?"

"Oh. I'm sorry. I didn't know I was."

Chestnut paused. "Well, is there?"

How could she say it? She had no explanation for it, and it sounded too absurd on its own. "I suppose I think too much," she said, brushing it off.

Chestnut glanced up. "Probably," she replied. "I believe you think too much if you're not all the way here. And you don't seem *quite* all the way here."

Luna closed the front cover of her book over her paw. "I do have trouble being here," she sighed.

"Truthfully, I don't *feel* all the way here, even though I'd like to be."

"What's the trouble?" Chestnut asked, pulling her brown thread through the stitching of a vine that was traveling across the fabric.

"I'm not sure …" Luna said. "I guess I wish being here with you—or even with myself, really—felt like it all went together. My memory … I just wish it all felt more … cohesive, I suppose."

"Cohesive," Chestnut repeated as she glanced up at her, then back to her intense concentration at her needlework.

Why did it sound so strange when spoken aloud? Luna shrugged and opened her book again. It was awkward, if not eerie, to piece apart.

"I'm listening," Chestnut assured her.

Luna began again. "Well … do you feel that everything connects? And that you're always right where you should be?"

Chestnut paused mid-stitch and frowned. "Perhaps …" she said, exhaling. "I don't know that I wake up in the morning wondering if everything connects," she said with an uptick in the corner of her mouth. "What doesn't connect?"

"I don't." *My footprints,* she almost said.

"What do you mean?"

Luna looked out the window at the snow on the

ground. "Every time the season changes, it feels as though it takes a part of me with it. It undoes everything that was planted or accomplished the season before. It may seem silly, but a season leaving always makes me feel left behind."

Chestnut's stitching slowed, though she looked at it ever as attentively. "Is there somewhere you would rather be?"

Luna frowned and thought for a moment. "I truly don't know. I'm just tired of feeling as though I need to leave."

"Well, for what it's worth, I'm glad you're here," Chestnut said, looking up at her. "I love my home, and I love the forest we live in, and I love that you're here."

"Thank you, Chestnut." Luna smiled at her.

Chestnut tidied up the table and put another log on the fire. Her delicate paws fluffed the pillows on the couch and reclining chair.

Luna dreaded leaving Chestnut's warm living room hearth. *This is the part,* she thought. *This is where they begin to disappear. It happens before I even leave.*

"I packed some bread for you in that cloth on the table," said Chestnut. "Will you be all right to walk in the snow? It's a shame I don't have a cot for you to sleep on."

"It isn't far," Luna replied, stretching at the hearth.

It's my leaving that does it, she thought, as she took the small parcel of bread from the table and put it in her satchel. She pulled her boots on at the door and wrapped her scarf around her neck and ears. She feared that she would disappear outside, as she suspected it happened somewhere at the threshold— many thresholds she'd left, for that matter.

Kissing on the cheek, they said their goodbyes. Except for the picket fence, the front yard was not distinguishable from the road with the fresh snow. Luna paused when she got to the road and looked down at her feet. They clearly were under the snow.

This precise ground has never been walked on, she thought. *When I pass, will it look exactly the same?*

She lifted her knee and looked down at the impression her foot had left. Her home now seemed a long way away. She made her way forward down the road keeping her arms close to her sides.

A squirrel lay underneath his fluffy tail in his hole atop an oak tree at the edge of the forest. His black eyes made out a rabbit walking by that night, barely noticeable against the white ground. Behind her lay a vast blanket of smooth, untouched snow.

Luna dreamed that night that she walked along the road carrying a bucket of glue and a paintbrush.

Tucked under one arm was a wad of paper-thin impressions in the shape of her feet. She slid one of the likenesses out from under her arm, dipped the brush into the bucket, and applied the clear glue to one side of it. Then she placed the print on the ground, smoothing it out evenly, only to have it slide around over the moist glue. After leaving it on the ground, the glue evaporated and the impression did not stick. While continuing to walk along, she tried this with dozens of other prints, only to have the same thing happen each time. The wind blew the prints away like leaves. By and by, she glanced down and noticed that the paintbrush had hardened, and moreover, that her bucket was empty.

EVERY SPRING, CHESTNUT went to visit her cousins who lived in another region of the forest. There would be new baby raccoons to meet: new nieces, nephews, second cousins, and first cousins once removed. She usually visited once a year in the warm months, and stayed for a number of weeks. She came by Luna's hut one morning to say goodbye before heading out.

"I should be back by June, July at the latest," she said. Luna began counting on her toes. "Of course it depends on how long we can all tolerate the same tree together."

"How many are in your family now?" Luna asked.

"About a thousand," Chestnut said with a chuckle. "If you ever need a change of pace, you're welcome to stay in my tree while I'm gone."

"Thank you. I'll just redecorate while I'm at it," Luna joked. They smiled at each other. Chestnut kissed Luna on both cheeks and headed out, and Luna walked her to the road.

Turning around and waving her tiny paw, Chestnut called, "Take care of Hickory. I'd hate to learn he's joined the circus when I get back."

"I wouldn't put it past him," Luna replied. She watched the road till Chestnut disappeared, then drew circles in the sand with her foot.

Hickory became somewhat agitated when winter left and the air began to smell of nectar. He had built a canoe over the winter and was eager to get it out on the water. He too needed to leave.

Luna knew he got this way every spring. Right around the beginning of April he started to breathe a bit faster, his whiskers stood up higher. When she visited him he dashed around his home opening too many cupboards and offering jam and bread while he spilled crumbs over the counters and floor. Luna smiled at the inevitable, but wished she could join wherever it was he decided he would go.

One day in late April, Luna saw a pair of furry legs walking with a green canoe overhead past her house.

She rushed outside and skidded to a stop on the road. "Hick! Where are you going?" she asked, out of breath.

He stopped and lifted the canoe above his head and set it down. A broad grin spread over his face from ear to ear. "Taking my boat out on her first excursion! I'm going all the way to the river and far beyond!"

"Right," she said, exhaling, not knowing what else to say. She noticed the backpack he was carrying. "Well, I just wanted to wish you a good trip."

"It's going to be a trip, all right! I'm rowing all the way down to the estuary. I'm determined to see the ocean this time. Do you know how many different fish and birds and frogs there are there?"

"Uh, no—"

"Sleeping out on the boat ... just me and the stars and the cranes and the water!"

"Oh, right. Yes, well, let me walk with you a bit. How long do you think you'll be gone this time?" she asked, steadying her breathing.

"It isn't about how long. If you think about time you miss out on things. I just need to be part of the water again. Did you know there are otters that live out in the sea? Imagine that!"

"They do? Well, yes, some do."

"They eat clams out in the open ocean. Just float-
ing on their backs out there," he said, chuckling.

Luna replied that she thought they ate fish,
and other meaningless responses in the vein of *ohs*
and *I sees*.

She accompanied him several miles until the
air grew cooler and damper, and mosquitos began
buzzing around them. The sun was ducking behind the trees.

"You might want to head back. It'll be dark by the
time you get home," Hickory said.

"All right," she sighed. Her whiskers twitched.
Hickory set the canoe on the ground.

"Come back by summer, okay, Hick?" she said, as
they embraced. "I'd hate to eat all the peaches without
you," she teased, trying to laugh.

She waited in the road for a while, watching his
figure get smaller. When she turned to go, a knot
formed in her stomach as she looked at the road they
had taken. Hickory's four-pointed hind footprints
stretched back as far as she could see. Hers were nowhere to be seen.

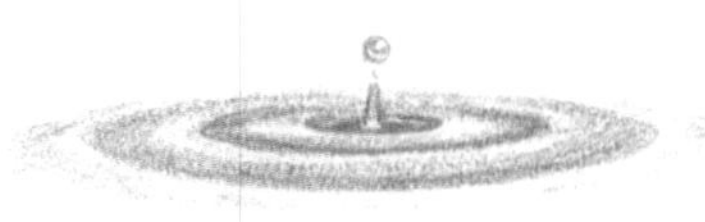

ights pass in silence. No creature could remember all their nights, when the wind howled or lay thick and still and hot. Attempting to account for all the nights of every creature combined would be like trying to count the leaves in a forest. Some slept, some tinkered away, some played, some worked, some dreamed. Some filled pages in private reverie, some whooped in the fields, calling out without being lost. Some tucked away their little ones, some prepared for little ones.

A million subtle changes happen over all those nights compounded. A million stories unravel one hair's breadth at a time, till each creature acquires his layers, and can recall his story only insofar as what mattered to him. Time, what a subtle thing—the difference between a seed and a tree with a hundred rings.

Luna wondered where all her nights went. In the morning—when perhaps the beans in the garden were noticeably plumper, or a flower's petals had opened—was she not also just a bit different? If she were, why, who would take notice? What witness had seen the nights before, watched the seed sprout underneath the earth?

She wondered during that spring and summer what would lessen the immensity of all those nights and days. If her time had been strewn away, lost its substance before it was complete, was there a place where it did not hang from her neck like a giant brass pendulum?

One night, as the days grew shorter and cooler again, Luna was washing dishes. Looking down at her hands in the water, an idea struck her.

My footprints won't show up in water, she thought. *I could go for a swim and see where that takes me.*

Having never gone swimming at night, especially alone, the idea should have terrified her. She wasn't sure that it didn't, yet the fear was less poignant in the face of her condition. Surely her dissolving footprints were more dreadful than a small sea of dark water, or even drowning, for that matter.

Luna had never been to the pond at night. She walked not fast, but purposefully. She shivered as a cool breeze rustled through the trees that skirted the pond. Their shadows covered the surface like giant hands. The body of water looked like a great black void in the middle of the forest. Swimming in that cold blackness seemed ghastly, though at least no one had footprints in water.

If she went in at all she would try to reach the bottom. To merely swim at the surface would serve no purpose other than to chill her to the bone. Were there any footprints at the bottom? Surely the water smoothed over the movement of the creatures who lived in it. She was a strong swimmer (albeit with her head above water), she could make it down.

It must go down awfully far, she thought. *Very far compared to how small I am. Ah, but to touch the bottom!* Even though her feet would not make prints on the ground where others walked, no one she knew had touched the bottom of the pond before.

She took off her coat and laid it on a bush on the bank. She waded in, then floated on her back, look-ing up at the stars framed by the treetops. It didn't matter here what she was or wasn't. The fish swam down in some world to which she gave no thought. They couldn't remember their lives, she supposed, nor should they. They swished their tails and the water did not retain their shape. Their lives were like their deaths—they were not to be remembered. Their home never allowed them to be more than a moment's refraction of light against a curved scale.

Luna swam down, her eyes shut tightly, then back up. She took another huge breath, then dove down again, beating her legs as fast as she could. Perhaps the weight of the water over her would help carry her down.

Hickory happened to be stargazing that night in his canoe at the far end of the pond. Lying supine with his head resting against his arms, his eyelids began to droop. He yawned and sat up, and began to row back across the pond.

As he neared the bank he noticed a peculiar object lying at the water's edge. It looked more and more like a creature as he approached. His curiosity mounted as he made out its wet fur. Luna sat up as she heard the ripples from his canoe approaching.

"Luna! Is that you?" Hickory exclaimed. "Good god! Why are you lying here?"

"I went for a swim."

Hickory stared at her nonplussed. "A swim— at this hour?" He paused for a moment. "Are you all right?"

"Do I look all right," she replied, though it was not a question.

He grabbed a woolen blanket from his canoe and wrapped it around her, drying off her fur. "Hold on." he stated. He pulled the canoe up onto the bank, then sat down facing her. "What is it, Luna? What are you doing here, really?"

"I thought I'd try to swim all the way to the bottom. I've never been there before."

"No one has, that I know of. Why would you want to?"

"My footprints are disappearing from the ground. It'd be better to be under water where no one has footprints."

"I don't understand," he said.

And she told him.

"Whatever has happened, you don't want to go down there," he said. "I've been down pretty far before. It's a long way. If you went too far you might not come back up."

"Is that so terrible?" she replied.

"Yes!" he declared. "You don't want to be down there. I want you here with us. It would be awful, for everyone ... " He tried to remind her of the forest. Surely so much beauty, so much potential, couldn't mean so little. How could she miss out on that? How could they miss out on her?

How true his words seemed. But the price for all of it seemed to be an indefinite amount of dark nights. How she ached to experience it without a care, but how unyielding her circumstance felt.

"I don't really want to go down forever," she admitted. "I just want to go to sleep until I'm all right."

Hickory told Luna to dry off and get warm at his home, and they walked swiftly back, their shoulders touching. They sat in front of a fire as her fur dried.

"It's as though whatever I do has never happened because my feet won't leave a trail," she said. "Wherever I go exists only in the moment I'm doing it." Looking around the room, she said, "It's as though … if I were one of your books, each page would get torn out as you read. When you got to the end there would be no book left, only a blank space."

He looked at her through furrowed brows. "This disappearing business is very serious indeed. When you first noticed that your footprints were not there, what did you do?"

"I kept walking, faster than I had before. All I wanted to do was get away from whatever was making them disappear."

"I see. But it seems you have not outrun that thing."

She paused. "No, I have not."

"I'm curious," he said, tugging at the fur on his chin. "You have not been able to run fast enough to keep your trail intact. Naturally, you've been running in the opposite direction. What do you suppose would happen if you ran into it?"

Luna stared at him. "What do you mean?"

"You've had dreams of being chased, haven't you?"

"Yes," she said tentatively.

"We always run away from whatever is chasing us in that dream. And we're usually just one step ahead of being caught by it. What would happen if we turned around and started chasing *it*?"

Luna turned her gaze to the fire. "Meeting fire with fire," she concluded.

"I guess that would be it."

"Well, I could experiment in my dreams, but this isn't a dream. This is *me*."

"Yes. The stakes are higher. You could certainly keep running from it."

"Don't you understand? I would disappear!" Her ears drooped on her shoulders.

"When you chase what you're running from you'll disappear?"

She nodded. "If there's nothing behind me, it's as though I hardly exist at all. How could what's left of me just run headfirst into some abyss?" She paused. "That's where everything goes that's silent and forgotten."

Hickory leaned forward and put his furry hand on hers. "You'd rather swim at the bottom of the pond than be estranged ... "

She looked at him through glassy eyes. Her nostrils flared out and back in, and she turned her nose toward the fire. A hot tear slid down her cheek and plopped on her fur. "I'd be gone all together. If I touched the bottom of the pond, at least I wouldn't know I was gone."

Hickory exhaled. "You're tired." He picked her white hand up and kissed it, then placed his hands underneath her elbows. "Stay here tonight. We'll both be here tomorrow morning."

A week later, an alarming knock rapped at Hickory's door in the morning. There stood Luna looking bewildered, wide-eyed and ears as stiff as boards.

"Luna!" Hickory exclaimed. "What's the matter? You look like you've seen a ghost!"

"Look," she admonished, extending her forearm. "I woke up this morning and noticed this."

"Come in," he beckoned, taking her arm and closing the door. "What is it?"

"Hickory ... look at me. Can't you see what I see? I'm fading. You can see through me."

Hickory merely looked puzzled. "Fading?"

"Come into the light," she said. She pulled him over to the window and let the morning light fall over her white fur. She held both arms out in front of her. Hickory looked dubious but examined them nonetheless. They stood in silence, both gazing down at her outstretched arms. At first, her fluffy white fur looked no different than usual.

"I don't understand," he said.

"Look!" she protested. "Look beyond my fur."

He acquiesced, his eyes adjusting, as if to view something in the distance. A pellucid view of his rug appeared through her arms, as though it were under water. Hickory's gaze rose up Luna's arm to her face. They stared at each other for several moments.

"I'm disappearing," she whispered.

Hickory touched Luna's arm. "I can still feel you. You're here now."

"I'll be gone soon," she said in a hoarse voice.

"Don't say that," he replied.

"It caught up with me. It erased all I've done, everywhere I've gone. And now—" she gazed again at the watery vision of his floor through her limbs.

Hickory placed his hands on her shoulders. "Listen to me. This *is* catching up with you. You have to chase it as fast as it has chased you."

Luna shook her head.

"I don't want to lose you," he added.

"I can't. The other side of this is the end of me."

"But where else can you go?"

"Hickory, I could only go if … " she paused and dropped her head. "Come with me. I couldn't manage it alone."

His hands slid down from her shoulders and he exhaled. "Alone is the only way."

"Why?" Luna felt her heart palpitating. Her body felt brittle.

"I would if I could," he began. "But I can't go with you. They're *your* footprints. You're the only one who can run back into them."

She backed away from him in dismay.

"Luna—" he began.

Brushing past him, she bolted through the yard and out the gate, feeling as weightless as a dry leaf. She glanced behind to see her footprints fading to flat ground. In a panic, she raced off the dirt path through a thicket, darting around trees in zigzag patterns, as though trying to dodge an owl about to snatch her in its clutches. She avoided looking down at her forefeet to see the brown foliage through them.

Where else can you go? Hickory's words echoed in her mind.

All day she ran without direction, hiding in empty burrows when she could run no more. She had no idea where she was, but it didn't matter. The destination was immaterial, only escape mattered.

The soil in the thicket gave way to rock. The view widened to a precipice. She sprinted to the edge before reversing and running back the way she had come. She made the loop five, six times. Her throat ached. *This is the only direction left to go,* she concluded. One last time she ran away from the precipice, farther than she had made the other strides.

You could keep going all the way home! she told herself with one last bit of false hope. *I have no home, and I will not disappear this way,* she resolved.

She winced, then darted back toward the cliff. The precipice approached quickly, and she might have collapsed had she run any farther. Leaping over the edge, the whole valley opened to meet her like cupped hands, as if to say, *Thank you.*

CHAPTER THREE

*L*una awoke to see dark green ripples, and heard waves lapping at a shore. She realized she was lying on the shoreline of a lake, though how she had gotten there she did not know. It didn't seem to matter much. Thirst overwhelmed her, and she crawled closer to the shore where she lapped up water until her tongue was sore. Her body ached and she felt as weak as the day she'd been born. This was not the bottom of the precipice. How had she gotten here?

Across the lake was a forest rolling into hills, then mountains, as far as the eye could see. The sun was low and cast golden rays on the turrets of a castle in the distance, peaking above the mountains surrounding them. It appealed to her immensely. Who lived there? A king and queen, an evil lord, or perhaps only cobwebs? While pondering this, she heard soft footsteps approaching. A doe walked toward her with her head bowed. Luna was relieved and pleased to see that she was not alone in this new place.

"Good evening," the deer greeted her.
"Are you well?"

Luna paused for a moment. "I—I don't think so. I
think I'm lost."

"Where have you come from?"

"From my home near the pond. But I don't
know how I got here. I jumped off a cliff and I
woke up here."

The deer's round eyes looked at her directly. "Yes,
I know where you've come from. Every once in a while
I meet a creature who has come from over there—not
very often."

"Well, I must be far from home, then.
Where am I?"

"You've come to the place you ran into. Where we
are now is very far away from the one you are familiar
with, but you are in the right place."

Luna agreed in silence. She had no desire to go
back, as she would have felt in any other unfamiliar
place. Where she wanted to go now was the castle in
the distance. "Do you know who lives in that castle in
the distance?" she asked, gesturing toward it.

"A great bear lives there," the deer replied. Her
voice trailed off at the end, almost nostalgically.

"A bear? Is he a lord?"

"You might say that."

Luna felt curious. She probed again. "A

king, then?"

"He could be. You might call him a sage, or he's a great teacher. No one knows how long he's lived there. Longer than any of us have been here. Whatever he is, he's the owner of the castle."

"Does anyone ever go there?" Luna asked tentatively.

The deer glanced down at Luna. "They do."

Luna sighed. "It must be very grand," she said, imagining pillared halls, telescopes and stacks of tomes, a bustling hub of creatures from foreign parts.

"It isn't," the deer stated.

Luna was caught off guard. "What do you mean? Don't scholars and statesmen come to meet with him?"

"It isn't those types of creatures that go to see him."

"Who, then?" Luna asked, puzzled.

"Those who have the will to go."

"What matters do they consult him on?"

"Oh, we would never know. Those things are only for the Bear and the one who goes."

Luna pictured making the journey to the castle. She longed to meet the Bear. Perhaps he could discern why her tracks disappeared, why *she* was disappearing altogether. More importantly, perhaps he could make visible all the tracks that were behind her.

"I need to go see this Bear. It's dreadful-
ly important."

"Yes, I know. All the animals who come from the
other side come to go to the castle."

"But I didn't know about the castle before I came.
I don't even know where I am now."

"You may not have known what was on the other
side, but that doesn't mean you weren't searching for
the castle."

Luna felt as though someone she'd never met had
called her by name. "Well, my matter is urgent. Could
you tell me the way?"

"You shall go see the Bear, but you must rest first.
You'll never make it as you are now. Climb on my
back," she said, bending down to the ground. "You can
stay with me until you're strong again."

Luna climbed up onto the deer's back, feeling con-
flicted over her exhaustion, and her urgency to find
the solution to her condition.

The deer stood up carefully and began walking
into the woods. "I'm Tamsen," the deer said, looking
back toward Luna. "What's your name?"

Luna told her and thanked her. There were a
few things she wanted to thank her for, but she laid
her head down on the deer's back without saying
anything more. She could not keep her eyes open,
and she hoped she would still be with Tamsen

when she awoke.

Luna awoke in a shaded wigwam. A couple open-
ings were carved in the side, from which she could
see birch branches swaying in the wind outside. Late
morning light flickered through the leaves and onto
her face. She thought of nothing else for a moment,
not where she was or whom she was with.

A carpet of grass covered the ground from wall to
wall and continued out the front opening. In the far
corner of the abode lay a round bed of crushed leaves
matted firmly together with the impression of its
owner. The home was otherwise empty.

Luna got up to eat breakfast growing outside.
(She did not think it was proper to eat the grass
growing inside.) The dwelling sat in the midst of a
birch grove. The trees' dappled leaf patterns swayed
over the grass. Luna spotted a familiar looking deer in
the distance, her head to the ground, eating breakfast.

"Tamsen! Hello!" Luna called as she hopped in
her direction.

"Good morning. It's good to see you up and well."

"I am well! Much better than last night. Thank
you so much for letting me stay. I need to be going
soon, though. I wanted to come say goodbye first."

The corners of Tamsen's mouth raised a fraction.
"I know how eager you must be to see the Bear, but

I wouldn't go so soon. You had a great fall yesterday. You fell asleep on my back as I walked home. You can rest here as long as you need. It will be quite a long journey to the castle."

"Thank you, but I just don't have a long time to spend doing other things. The very reason I'm here is because I couldn't wait any longer. I must go as soon as I can."

"Yes, you *should* go as soon as you can, my friend. And not a moment too soon. I would advise you to save your strength to make it the whole way. It would do no good for you to perish before you arrive because you didn't have the strength to go on."

Luna considered Tamsen's advice. She may have mistaken urgency for energy, and had tried to start out with too little.

She stayed with Tamsen for a short season, not wandering too far from the wigwam in the birch grove. At night they watched the sun slip down through the treetops and the stars come out.

One night they lay in the grass near the wigwam gazing at the stars.

"Tamsen … I'm so glad you asked me to stay, for now," Luna said.

"I'm glad you decided to stay. It isn't just the long journey that requires your true energy; it's all the decisions along the way. You need your full heart and mind for those. You must consider all things carefully."

"Do you think it's easy to get lost out there?"

"Without the strength, yes. It becomes easy to give up. The trees grow very thick in some places. It may be hard at times to tell your direction even during the day. You need your full self to keep your scent and your wits about you."

Tamsen suggested they go to the little pond near her wigwam to get a drink before heading inside. Luna rode on Tamsen's back as she walked along the narrow trodden path toward the water. Ripples float-ed across the black water as they drank, scattering the faint reflection of starlight. Luna recalled the night at the pond with Hickory. She dipped her foot in, pon-dering how everything became the same in water.

Tamsen waded into the pond, submerging her face several times and shaking the water off her body.

"I might go tomorrow," Luna said. "I think I'm ready."

"All right," Tamsen replied. "Remember, the Bear's castle is west of here. Don't travel at night. You can follow the sun throughout the day, but find safety when it starts to set. I know you'll find it."

"Thank you," Luna said.

Tamsen beckoned Luna out into the water, only up to Tamsen's belly, but swimming depth for Luna.

She paddled out, then went under and emerged next to Tamsen. Tamsen tucked her legs under her and lay down in the water.

Climbing up on Tamsen's back, Luna asked, "Tam, how long have you lived?"

"Ten years," she replied.

"In your wigwam?"

"Well, I didn't always live in the wigwam, but here in this forest."

"And you knew you were supposed to be here?"

"I couldn't be anywhere else. I'm part of this forest. My breath is the same as the trees. When I walk alone in the woods, deeper than the birches, the trees speak to me. I'm with them."

"What do they say?"

"It's like a long loving greater than words. How can I express it?"

"That sounds wonderful ... but strange. It almost sounds lonely."

"Oh no, never. It's the opposite of lonely. It's being. It's my home. When I'm among the great ones, the ones who have been here ten of my lifetimes, I look up at their canopy as if I were a tree, and they see me. That silence, being loved by trees and their roots, that is fullness."

Luna quivered, from the moistness of her fur or something else, she wasn't sure. "That sounds like pure bliss. I would love to belong to trees like you do."

"Did you not belong to the trees in your forest?" Tamsen asked.

Luna exhaled in something like a laugh and a shiver. "I'm cold," she stated.

"Come, let's go back," Tamsen said, and she stood up.

The next morning, Luna asked Tamsen to take her to where the trees spoke to her. She planned to leave, but not before she could see Tamsen's sanctuary. They traveled miles, Luna riding on Tamsen's back. Tamsen walked with purpose for a long time. As the birches became fewer and gave way to larger trees, she slowed her stride. She placed each hoof softly on the ground, in silence.

"Luna, climb down," she said. "Touch the ground yourself." Tamsen knelt down and Luna climbed off. She heard nothing but her own breath. Kapok trees stood tall and patient and still. Their buttressed roots clung to the soil like waves stuck in time. Though it was daytime, the sunlight did not penetrate the canopy of leaves. What little light there was was but a dim green glow.

"This is where I'm home," Tamsen said. "I'm part of these trees in the same way they are part of each other, and separate from them in the way they are separate from each other. One day I'll be underneath these trees. They'll hold me in their roots, and I may become a part of their leaves or moss or bark. I won't be separate from them at all."

They stood a while in stillness, saying nothing. Luna heard the beat of her heart. She looked up and saw Tamsen with her head turned toward the tree-tops, eyes closed. She had never seen another creature so enraptured, so completely belonging to another, as she was seeing Tamsen now.

"Do they say anything to you?" Luna asked.

The deer opened her eyes. "Sometimes we don't need words. They know I belong here, that I'm part of them. And we need nothing else."

"Thank you for showing me your home," Luna said. "I would love to belong here in the way you do," she added.

"I want you to belong to yourself, here in this forest or anywhere else," Tamsen said.

"Thank you. I know you do. I don't know exactly what that means, but from you, it means the world."

And she kissed Tamsen's nose and went west.

SHE TRAVELED FOR several days. The earth gave way to a blanket of moss that covered the forest floor. Mounds like green balloons billowed over the ground, and gumdrop patches grew up tree trunks. A dull hum in the trees grew louder each night, though Luna could not place where it was coming from. The hum grew to a roar before she realized it was not the trees, but tens of thousands of cicadas, crawling and flying among the trees. Their song reverberated around the forest, rising and falling like a deafening snore.

While resting to stretch and groom her face and ears, she heard a small voice chirp, "Good evening!" Looking up, she saw a cicada with glossy brown wings perched on a nearby tree trunk, waving a skinny arm in greeting.

"Good evening," Luna replied.

"What type of animal are you?" the cicada asked.

Luna furrowed her eyebrows and extended an ear forward inadvertently. "A rabbit," she provided.

"A rabbit. Hmm, pleasure to meet you. I'm a cicada."

"Have you recently moved here?" Luna asked, curious about the cicada's ignorance.

"Oh no. I've lived here all my life, but I've been underground for seventeen years—ever since I was born! I came up into the wide world only a few days ago."

Luna was stunned. "So, this is all new to you ... the stars and the trees and the air. What were you doing all that time under the earth?"

"Oh, I crawled among the roots of trees, mainly to eat and grow up."

Luna couldn't fathom seventeen years, much less seventeen years in a dark place. It was much longer than she would ever live. "I've climbed in burrows, but only for a day or so," Luna said. "Some hot days I've napped in a cool burrow, but there's too much up here. I love the creatures and the ponds and the sky, even the mud—all of it! In all that time, didn't you want to come up and see the world?" she asked.

"Well, no, but all of us cicadas do the same. We hatch in our nests in the trees and then jump from the branches right into the ground on the day we're born. We live underground for years until we're ready to lay our eggs. I was always looking forward to having little ones."

"You mean you waited all this time underground for children?" Luna asked in quiet amazement.

"Yes. It was quite some time, but now that I'm in the wide world—it's lovely here!—my mate and I nuzzle under the moonlight at night. We're expecting some of our own soon!"

"Wonderful, I wish you all the best with yours." Just then Luna noticed a transparent husk the exact likeness of the cicada stuck on the tree trunk a couple feet above the insect.

The cicada followed Luna's eyes up to the husk and commented, "Why, that's my shell up there. I wiggled out of it not a week ago. It's been a long life,"

she said with a sigh. "But soon I'll climb right back
up the trunk of this tree and lay my eggs before I
say goodbye."

"Goodbye? Goodbye already? Why, you only just
came out of your husk!"

"That's true. But after all, I've lived even longer
than you, I bet."

"Yes, but—" Luna felt desperate, but afraid to
offend the creature. "All those years … you were never
seen. Not that living underground is bad—I—I'm
sure of course, it must be grand. But couldn't you have
lived up here with the sky and the trees? You said
you love it here. Why … so long? Seventeen years *is*
longer than I've lived—longer than I'll *ever* live. Did
you really have to hide for so long to be able to shed
your skin?"

"*We* do. I don't know about other creatures."

Luna sat before her in silence with a hollowness
in her stomach. An unfathomable amount of time it
took to grow up, it seemed, especially when this tiny
creature would leave it all after such a brief time.

*L*una parted ways with the cicada and continued across the mossy forest floor. One evening a bright color in her periphery caught her eye. She looked to the side, and saw a large pink silk moth resting near the bottom of a tree trunk. Its coral wings lay wide open. On its hind wings were two orange circles like eyes, encircled by magenta rings. They seemed to stare boldly into hers. Luna had never seen anything so exquisite in her life. She was afraid to speak for fear it would fly away.

"Hello," she whispered. The moth's wings folded together slowly and opened again. Luna blinked and gulped. "You're so ... lovely."

The moth fluttered its wings and hovered in mid-air, then flew up the tree trunk.

"Oh! I'm sorry," Luna called after it, but it flew higher into the branches. She sat disgruntled and embarrassed on the ground, feeling rather ordinary. She began grooming herself, tugging on her ears a bit harder than usual.

A rabbit speaking to a silk moth … imagine.
She cringed.

As she hopped along the blanket of moss, another silk moth appeared, then another. One after another, then dozens, all resting on the trunks of trees. Luna came to a large beech tree where they congregated like bees to a hive. The pink moths covered the tree by the thousands. Neither the trunk nor the leaves could be seen. Thousands of magenta eyes blinked and stared at her. An ethereal pink glow emanated from inside the leaves. It looked warm and quiet and safe.

At the base of the tree, the magenta eyes of a moth blinked at her. "May we help you?" it asked.

"What's inside there?" Luna asked, staring up at the tree.

"That's where our baby moths are born. We help keep them warm by surrounding the tree."

Luna considered then that she did not know where or when she had been born. Maybe rabbits are born in burrows or in hollow logs … but how long ago? She didn't know. The realization was perplexing. How could one not know how one was born? It was like suddenly forgetting one's own name. Was it possible to live yet never have been born? It was absurd. But after all, so was disappearing.

"How long does it take for them to be born?"

Luna asked the moth.

"Days, weeks, as long as they need. We just keep them warm until they do."

She felt a fire kindle in her chest to see inside the tree, to see how a thing is born. Did it not take more than the warmth of a hundred thousand moths' wings to be born? It seemed to be the most effortful thing in the world, she reasoned. Perhaps she was disappearing because she had never been born. "I've never seen anything be born before," she said. "I don't even know how *I* was born," she added quietly.

"Well, perhaps you've come to the right place," replied the moth. "Stay here," it said as it joined the other moths among the leaves.

The sea of moths parted in two like a giant curtain, hovering in midair, to reveal a globular pink room inside the tree. The glow beamed out into the evening, falling on the ground. Thousands of white cocoons hung to the lining of the inner orb, each one like a crystal on a great chandelier. In the center hung an immense crystalline cocoon, five times Luna's size. It trembled, cracked open, and from it emerged a snowy white silk moth, its pulsating body looking like a dry leaf. With each inhalation, its wings became straighter. Two feathery yellow plumes swayed from the top of its head. It flapped its wings as they became as flat as boards. Luna felt the wind from the moth's wings on her face.

The snow-white queen moth then fluttered her wings and landed like a feather on the edge of the room in the tree. "Did I hear you say you'd never seen anything be born?" the moth addressed her.

"Until now, Your Highness," Luna replied in awe. It seemed only appropriate to call this creature this title, for she certainly must be the queen moth. And yet she'd only just been born.

"The cocoon is difficult to break through, but one doesn't have a choice. I'd suffocate if I stayed in there forever. And I must show the others how to come out. And you, child, you cannot remember where you were born?"

"Your Majesty, I am not so sure that I have been born at all."

The queen nodded thoughtfully. "What is your name?"

The queen considered Luna's response with a smile. "Why, what a wonderful name! Ah, Luna, the moon! You've been born and reborn for eternity. You wax and wane, burgeoning over and over with each new phase."

"I'm honored, Your Majesty. I wish I were like the moon, indeed. Truthfully, I don't know where or when I was born. I confess, I wish so badly to be born, and to know I had been born."

The queen's iridescent green eyes softened, and she fluttered her wings. "Come, you must come in-side," and she drifted down to Luna on the ground. "Climb on my back."

Luna wiggled up onto the moth's thorax, getting a fine, glistening dust all over her coat. The queen flew back into the tree and the curtain of pink moths closed behind them. The floor of the globe was a huge cushion, exquisitely soft, deep, and slightly damp.

Luna learned the birthing process of the queen moth. Every few weeks she built a cocoon in the cen-ter of the tree, in the midst of the other tiny cocoons. There she waited along with the others before making her arduous egress. How many times she had done this she had never counted.

"If anyone were like the moon, Your Majesty, it would be you. You've been born more times than you know, whereas I have no idea ..." she trailed off. At the queen's request, Luna told her everything that had happened before she had come upon the tree. "Even now, I can see the cushion of your lovely room straight through my feet." Luna said.

"One does want to be concrete," the queen said. "It's easier that way. But that isn't the way. It isn't our way, or the moon's way, or the forest's way. You keep changing no matter what. You may be afraid of dis-appearing, but you'll find by and by that you expand when you're not attached to what you're aching to be."

"Your Majesty, I believe you in my heart, but how can I stop wanting?"

"Oh, that is the great question. Child … that is the question." Her gossamer eyes glistened. "When these pupas here are caterpillars, they're caterpillars. No amount of wanting makes them moths. But they release their form when it's time. You also must release who you convinced yourself you were before—even the you that's fading away."

"If you only knew how much I am aching to make myself be where I am—to materialize!"

"I do," the queen replied.

"Forgive me, Majesty. I know you do—more than anyone. It's just … I'm an animal too! I'm *here*."

"Yes, yes, you are. You *are*."

"If I stopped wanting all that I do, how could I change?"

"The changing isn't in the wanting, dear. Trust me. Let's not want for a moment, and you'll find you are so much more than your obsession."

The queen extended a delicate arm to Luna, and with a flutter of her wings, lifted her off the floor and flew to the top of the dome. With her two forearms, she pulled a silk string from her abdomen and hung it from the top of the room. At the bottom of the string she began to spin a cradle of white silk, whirling it like a lump of clay on a wheel.

"This is for you," she said, as she lifted Luna into the cradle. "When I'm in my cocoon, I do not think about coming out. I don't even think about before. I look at one place each moment. The only thing that is still me is my lungs expanding and shrinking. If you want to know what's real, it's only this moment. Breathe in. That's who you are. Breathe out. That is you."

Neither spoke for a moment. Luna observed her soft breath coming in and leaving. *This. And this. And this. And this.*

The queen flapped her wings, making the cradle sway. "Look the moon in the eye," she whispered. "You won't fade away. You'll discover everything you really are. You'll be free." She flew upward and spread her wings flush against the top of the dome. "Make room!" she called, and the moths at the top of the tree flew aloft. White moonlight flooded in and beamed through her wings, illuminating her veins.

The cocoons hanging around the room swayed and began to break open. Damp and wrinkled moths struggled out and beat their wings, clinging to their former dwellings as they dried. After a while, having discovered their new form, the new pink moths fluttered around the room, some landing on Luna's nose and ears.

"Oh my ... you're lovely," she tittered in delight.

"Make room!" the queen called again from the top. The curtain of moths parted and the young moths flew out into the night sky. Luna watched them disappear into the dark.

"Your Highness, they're gone! I want to go too!" she choked up. "Let me change too!"

The queen called down to her, "Luna, look at the moon! Look into his eyes until he is all you see."

The moths surrounding the tree came back together, leaving an opening framing the moon. Luna peered into his right eye gazing at some distant star. She hung in her silk cradle and fell asleep with the grooves of giant craters reflecting in her eyes like glass.

The next morning the queen moth came to lift Luna from the cradle. The moths that had surrounded the tree had flown away, and only a veil of leaves remained. Sunlight flickered through tiny spaces.

The queen fluttered over to a stout stone console with an amethyst top at the side of the room. Luna had not noticed it the night before. A silver jewelry box encrusted with crystals rested on its surface. The queen opened its lid and pulled out a hinged oval case of gold. Opening the case, she produced a golden brown tulip bulb.

Turning to Luna, she said, "I've saved this bulb for

one I know will find the right home for it." She then lifted a suede drawstring bag from the jewelry box's drawer and placed the bulb in it. "This is for you. Plant this bulb where it will thrive, where it will mean the most to you. I trust you will find the right place."

"Thank you so much, your Highness. I'm honored to have it." Luna slipped the bag over her shoulders.

The queen carried Luna on her back out of the tree and as far as she could physically bear her weight, before bringing her safely to the ground. Luna hopped off, covered in shimmering dust.

"Oh, I can never thank you enough," she said, turning to face her.

The queen flapped her wings and ascended off the ground, blowing her dust off Luna's fur. "My dear, one more thing: when you can't stop wanting, let that part in too!" And she flew up into the sky and disappeared.

CHAPTER FIVE

*L*una headed west each day. At first she kept
track of the days since she'd left the moths: it
had been three weeks and five days—no, four, possi-
bly. Four weeks or five. Now definitely a month? Six
weeks, most likely.

Trees grew further apart and grass became sparse
and brown. She could follow the sun more directly
this way, but it also made the journey unpleasant with
less shade. The weather grew hot and the dry air she
breathed in felt as though it had come out of an oven.

One day there wasn't a cloud in the sky or the
slightest breeze blowing. Luna furrowed her eyebrows
in the unforgiving sun. It had been too long since she'd
had water and she cursed her warm coat.

As she stopped for a rest under a bony tree, a ra-
ven landed nimbly on a branch above her. It cawed as
it found its footing and tilted its head to stare at her.
Luna glanced up at the newcomer. Its eyes were like
black glass beads, hostile yet vacant. She cleared her

throat, giving the unnerving bird a chance to speak, if it could. It merely let out another deep caw that made Luna uneasy.

She began to move on, assuming the bird to be without speech, when it let out another alarming caw. Two more ravens joined it, all cawing over one another. Luna felt a strong impetus to get away, and was surprised when the birds followed her.

"What do you want?" she clamored. "I have no food! Go bother someone else! Off with you!"

Yet they swooped lower and lower, intimidating her with their cries. "Caw! Caw! Caw!" they cried incessantly, till it began to sound like *Lost! Lost! Lost!*

To Luna's dismay, several more ravens joined the posse, elevating the harassment to torment. With each swoop they pecked at her, ripping off tufts of fur and cawing in guttural sounds, "Lost! Lost!"

Luna shrieked in terror and pain. Just ahead was a slotted granite crag. She raced toward it, hoping to find a crevice to hide in. Squeezing swiftly through a slot, she evaded the tormentors. Flying in circles, they continued to call out from the top of the rocks, "Lost! Lost!"

Her heart was racing. As she inhaled air in gulps, she felt the sting of her sweat dripping into the punctures their beaks had made. Tufts of white fur and specks of blood were strewn in the sand where she'd dove in.

"Are you hurt?" a soft voice called from further inside. She turned to see an elderly tortoise making her way toward her.

"Yes—no," she replied, steadying her voice.

"Child, you are! I woke up to some racket. What happened?"

Luna recalled the strange and chilling events.

"Oh my," the tortoise said. "Well, stay here, at least for a while. It's cooler in here. Those brutes nicked you pretty good," she said, examining Luna's fur.

Luna sat in the sand and preened her fur, mainly to calm herself. The tortoise remained quiet for a while, then asked, "Are you indeed lost?"

Luna thought for a moment, then replied, "Yes, I am."

The tortoise looked deeply at Luna, an infinite patience in her eyes. She nodded slowly.

"Why they terrorized me like they did, I don't know," Luna added in the silence.

"*They* don't matter much. Tell me now, are you merely lost, or are *you* lost?"

Luna furrowed her eyebrows, puzzled. The tortoise looked back at her patiently. "What do you mean?" Luna asked.

"I'd like to know, do you not know where to go, or did you lose *you*?"

Countless footprints came to her mind, a long journey that lacked continuity. The whole journey was somehow without a history, its very essence. "I lost a lot of pieces. They happened somewhere, but I don't know where they are. It isn't just the pieces though— it's me." Luna told her about jumping off the precipice the day she started disappearing. "You must think I'm crazy," she said in the tortoise's silence.

"Far from it," the tortoise replied. "What do you suppose this disappearing wants?" she asked.

What on earth could it want? It had never occurred to her. Luna thought of the first time she spoke with Hickory about her disappearing; how, as in a nightmare, she had always run away from it. *What would happen if you ran into it?*

"I'm afraid of what it wants," Luna admitted.

"Of course! You did what anyone would do. Running is the safest bet. This old shell would've been swallowed up for sure! I just wonder … did you pay it any mind from the beginning?"

"I couldn't! When I looked back and didn't see any footprints, I panicked. I ran away!"

The tortoise patted Luna's foot. "Anyone would, dear. Something I wonder though, is how pernicious this thing was. What if you had given it your attention?"

Luna thought as the tortoise continued. "Why, I

think of how hungry I've gotten out here in this des-
ert. I wake up in the morning and my stomach looks
forward to some nice grub. I don't think much of it
as long as I find one. My stomach starts out real nice
to me. I start imagining the tasty things it would like.
Then it gets cranky when it doesn't get them. Some
days I've found no crickets, no berries, not anything.
Hunger goes from real polite to an angry beast in a
matter of time. There's nothing wrong with hunger,
it just doesn't like being ignored. Something tells me
this thing didn't like being ignored either."

"Yes, perhaps." Luna considered all the seasons
that had passed in her home, the slow but persistent
gnawing she felt inside. In all that time, she had had
an uneasiness she had both nursed and neglected.

The tortoise fed her a supper of crickets and dried
berries. Luna had never met any creature so simple
or humble. She slept in the tortoise's rocky home,
and whispered her thanks and goodbye at dawn the
next morning.

By and by the arid sand gave way to foliage yet again.
She was protected from the sun's rays and birds of
prey, yet she did not feel safe. There was a different
type of density to this forest than where she had left
Tamsen. It was shadowy, the air was thick and leaden,
with moss and brush in every crevice. No creatures

rambled about. None but one.

Luna noticed a furry tawny body that lay perched in a tree some thirty feet away. This creature, a caracal, lounged on its side upon a branch licking the pads of its paw luxuriously. Luna's heart stopped. She made a painstaking move underneath a bush. The feline made no sign that she had seen Luna, even though she must have been the only thing moving within the vicinity. Luna sat still as a stone, wondering how long before the cat would leave.

The caracal finished cleaning her paw, then stretched her forelegs forward and yawned, revealing teeth that made Luna dizzy.

"You needn't hide down there so still and silent," the cat declared in a regal voice, looking up as though she hadn't seen Luna at all. "Come out and chat. I've spoken to no one all day or the day before."

Luna didn't move a muscle. Even the air seemed to hang motionless like a taxidermied head on a wall.

"You suppose I'm going to eat you," she snickered. "Naturally. But I'm not hungry at the moment. Come out, little thing." She finally lowered her hazel eyes toward Luna, locking gazes with her. "Who are you?"

Several moments of silence passed before Luna responded. The one word was swallowed up in the dead space.

"Luna," the cat repeated. "You might as well come

out from hiding." Her tail flicked gently back and forth from where it hung off the branch. Luna had no choice. Her limp legs took two steps forward out from under the bush.

"Tell me, what business are you engaged in this evening?" the cat asked.

"On my way to the Bear's castle," Luna croaked.

The caracal's tail stopped. "Oh, you're not from around here … you've come to see the Bear," she remarked with a wry grin. "Why?" Her grin fell.

"To sort out a problem."

"And what would that be?"

Luna wondered if she should lie, though she couldn't think of any other dilemma, and she couldn't refuse to answer. "Some things are happening … that I can't control. The Bear will know."

The caracal stretched again and dragged her claws across the tree branch, leaving white claw marks. "Oh yes, the Bear will know," she said sardonically.

Luna wondered how long this would last—how long *she* would last.

"You needn't trouble yourself with such an arduous trip. You won't find what you're looking for."

How would you know? thought Luna.

"What is, is what will be," said the feline, then swooped some fifteen feet to the ground with ease. "What exactly is the matter so pressing you needed to come so far away from home?"

Luna was beginning to realize creatures like herself were well-known here. "I'm disappearing," she said.

The cat looked at her with a cold apathy. "Yes, you are. I thought you looked strange under that bush. And so this Bear is going to … ?"

"I … don't know," Luna replied.

"Hmm, yes." With one claw she drew lines in the dirt, looking casually at her claw marks. "Luna, Luna … you think the Bear is the oldest creature here. I've lived in the forest as long as he's lived in the castle. You don't know that, I know. I've seen creatures like you pass through, though nothing happens, really." She advanced one step forward. "Tell me, is the problem that everyone can clearly see you're disappearing or that no one can?"

Luna's mouth was dry. Her head was buzzing. "Isn't disappearing enough of its own problem?" she replied.

"Indeed it is. And it's plain to me that you have that problem. But let me save you time." She took another step forward. "Accept your disappearance now because your condition will only worsen. If only you small, sad creatures could accept what is. This isn't going to get easier."

"I'll die fighting." Luna tried to sound convicted,

but she knew the cat was right.

"I believe you. But, this disappearing ... is that merely your problem, or is that what you are?"

"The B—"

"—Bear will know, yes, of course," the cat finished. "I can tell you what *I* know. You barely exist. I see no path behind you—just a ghost in front of me."

An icy feeling passed over Luna's body like a specter. It took her breath away. The cat lowered onto her haunches and Luna bolted toward a thicket of thorny brambles. The caracal leapt after her. Thorns pierced Luna as she maneuvered between the vines, but the feline stopped at the front, pawing through the spaces and baring her fangs.

Luna cowered in her pocket of safety as the gaze of the cat's hazel eyes pierced into hers from the outside.

"Many before you have been lost without a trace in this forest!" the cat hissed. "The cicadas creep under the ground and the badgers crawl into their burrows. I sit in my tree and I see them all. You float through the trees like a phantom. No one knows where you've been. You have no nest or burrow or hole. I see you, and you float away." The cat let out a shrill scream that shattered the stale air, then departed.

Luna waited. And waited. It seemed like an eternity until she realized she was breathing again. She painstakingly crawled through the rest of the brambles and out the other side, still shaken. Her fur was streaked with thorn marks and specks of blood.

A pond lay near where she emerged and a full moon reflected on its surface. Coming to the water's edge, she peered down at her reflection and pondered how close to death she had just come. Death itself seemed unexpected and perplexing. She did feel very much like a phantom, as the caracal had said. But how much can a phantom die? She had thought death would be an instantaneous change in form. Yet it seemed now that it was like a fading flame being carried away in the dark, or like watching a bird fly into the sky until it disappeared.

She looked out at the moon's reflection rippling on the water and its ivory glow in the sky. *How can a creature as small as I feel so greatly alone?* she wondered in bewildered awe.

When the goldfinch cannot sing,
When the poet is a pilgrim,
When prayer will do us no good.
"Traveler, there is no path,
The path is made by walking."

Joan Manuel Serrat

*L*una's tender physique changed with time. Her plump cheeks hollowed, and her round thighs shrank and grew taut. She remembered the days when she met in the fields with Chestnut and Hickory, picnicking under a tree or going for a swim in the pond. It was there in her memory, though like a dream. It had been a long time since she had met any other animals with speech. She could hardly remember how long it had been since she had spoken.

Speech did not seem necessary anymore. There was nothing left to say. She had tried to keep track of time at the beginning, but moments had all blurred together. Words dissolved in fatigue or renunciation.

She heard the patter of her feet on the ground, though she did not look behind her anymore. She often wondered why she continued searching for the castle—which at times seemed to be a useless conquest—and make a new burrow here.

She stopped near a shallow pool and saw her

gaunt reflection in it. Sunken cheeks, frayed whiskers, thinning fur, and distant eyes looked back at her. It was as though she were looking at another rabbit, rather than her own reflection. But she felt nothing. Presently a squirrel skittered to the pond to wash its face, causing ripples across the water. Looking up, he waved at Luna. "Hello! Cool weather!" he called.

Luna understood the words but sat unresponsive, without thought.

The squirrel tilted his head with an inquisitive grin. "Do you live near here?" he asked.

Nothing.

The squirrel's expression changed, as though he realized he was speaking with a speechless animal. He then gamboled away.

Luna turned numbly toward a patch of bulrushes by the edge of the pond and began to eat the stalks. Lying down afterward, pain rumbled around in her stomach. She felt a hard ball pitted in the center of her belly for a while. Perhaps the mass inside her intestines had encountered a wall; or perhaps her insides were not of the integrity she had had before she came here. Had she turned into a dark, empty jar, where the things she ingested would plop to the bottom without metabolizing? Perhaps the matter she needed for survival was lodged in its place, unable to be taken apart. She heaved involuntarily and vomited.

She felt nothing, not even disgust, as she wiped her mouth on the grass and turned away from the vomit.

She continued walking in the same direction and began traveling up a steep incline for several miles. The sun began to set. Pine trees skirted along the east side of the mountain, and a narrow break in the trees opened to overlook the valley below. She took the path through the break in the trees to see how far she had come. Where was the lake she had arrived at? It was long gone now.

A flock of birds flew through the sky. Hundreds swerved back and forth in unison, dancing in the sky. She watched the murmuration billowing and collapsing across the sky. Two lines of birds trailed away from the mass. A slope protruded from the middle and a horizontal curve formed near the bottom. The corpus took the form of a feminine face with flowing hair. Eyelashes of thick birds' wings opened, and an enormous pair of brown eyes opened and looked at her. A faint smile formed on the woman's face. She exhaled and a breeze blew through the trees.

"Where are you from?" the woman asked her. Luna merely looked down.

"Where are you going?" she inquired again.

"Where I would like to go and where I am going may not be the same thing."

"May I help you?" she asked.

Luna rested her head on her forefeet. How useless it all seemed: seeking the Bear or seeking help. Perhaps just finding a new home in this forest, bewitched as it may be, was her task. Was this all there was to hope for?

She looked into the woman's eyes. Her journey seemed too convoluted to recall, and her ability to tell it worn down. "I was looking for a Bear. But it doesn't matter," she said.

"You've been searching for a long time?"

They locked gazes but Luna said nothing.

"I understand," the woman said. "So many pieces of me have flown apart for miles," she said, turning around and looking out toward the horizon. "Across the mountains, in forests, over the sea. We birds have seen all the travelers in every trail and corner. We're travelers ourselves. Sweet rabbit ... you are not alone."

A single sparrow from the woman's form flew down and alighted on Luna's shoulder. She felt a tepid glow of gratefulness, and opened her mouth. "Your birds see all us tiny creatures roaming here on the ground. What good is it? Are we all nomads, or do some find their burrows for their short season before they say goodbye?"

A breeze picked up. It whistled through the trees, dragging leaves off the cliff with it. Some birds broke away from the woman's form and flew away.

"I've asked for too long. I can't ask anymore," Luna said. "Do the others get to where they're done with words, done trying to make others understand, done willing to find their way?"

"Why, yes! We birds have flown through every branch, lived in every tree. You are not alone."

"I've said all the words till talking seems pointless—even to myself. I haven't spoken in so long. I can't listen anymore either."

"That may seem like the dead end of a long road," the figure said, "but only if it gives birth to despair. The silence that comes after a winding path may be the beginning of a different path. Silence is a path too."

"I don't want any more paths. I just want to be home."

"Silence may be a way there." Her voice sounded as though it were coming from all directions. "Embrace this silence," she whispered.

Luna winced. "How can I embrace something so hollow?"

"Consider the silence of snow in a deep wood, the silence of the stars and moon, a leaf's blood flowing through its veins. Words will fail to tell you where you are, fail to tell others. Allow the silence. Wait for who you are there."

The flock of birds rose higher and farther away,

and the woman's form dissipated. In the wind, her last words were barely audible. "Sweet rabbit, you needn't be other than what you are. You can be."

Luna walked that night, and the next and the next. Even during the day, it was difficult at times to follow the sun's direction. The ground was shadowy, and she would often lose sight of where the sun was in the sky. She walked on in silence, never looking behind her, afraid of the untrodden path she would see.

One night, where the trees grew dense, Luna could barely see the path in front of her. It had become dark quickly, and she realized her error in not finding a burrow sooner. The silhouettes of the trees were barely visible against the night sky, and the darkness pervaded her surroundings until she could not see her own feet. She breathed in and out, wondering what else to do besides stay put all night.

There in the dark, a glow appeared in the distance above her. It grew, materializing into a woman. Her blond hair cascaded over her white robe. Her striking green eyes looked down at Luna. "Luna," the woman spoke, leaning forward.

"Here I am," Luna said.

"You're weary," she stated.

"Yes."

"Come with me. I'll carry you home."

"Who are you?" Luna asked.

"I am the great home, the last door every creature opens. You looked for me in your pond but I'm here now. Crawl into my arms. You don't have to walk anymore." She held out her arms.

The fragrance of a flower wafted into Luna's nostrils. The aroma was soothing, intoxicating, and made her long to follow the woman. Just then, it turned on her tongue to the bitter taste of a rose she had chewed and spat out when she was young. The taste nearly made her retch, and she spat out her acrid saliva. "I don't want you," she grimaced through tears.

"But you do, Luna," the woman corrected her.

"I don't *want* to want you," she sobbed. "I don't want the bitterest rose to eat because it was the only thing left to eat."

"I understand … but how much longer do you have to walk? Can you make it?"

It was impossible to say. Suppose she reached the castle the next morning. But suppose it was nowhere near. Suppose the Bear couldn't help her at all. Suppose she disappeared before she arrived. Nothing could be determined.

"I don't know," she admitted. "But I can't go on forever." And she wept.

"Luna, Luna," the woman cooed. She reached her hand down to stroke Luna's face and ears. "You need rest. I will carry you with me. Is that not what you want?"

Luna felt an overwhelming pull inside of her towards the woman, a yearning that felt like a cord was attached to her, bringing her closer to the woman's arms. Her feet were planted on the ground, yet her hands were placed in the soft palms of the woman. Tamsen's words then came softly to her mind: *Consider all things carefully.*

"I want who I was supposed to be when I didn't want you," she resolved.

Just then the woman and her light disappeared. The stars came out at that moment and Luna could see through the night. Their staggering number radiated in a deep blue sky. She could see now that she was looking out over a wide valley. A breeze picked up and blew coldly against the tear trail on her face. She looked out and saw the undulating horizon of mountains on the other side rising to meet the expanse of sky.

The chasm that lay between her and the horizon filled her whole mind. A boundless space expanded inside her. Her mind was empty. There were no words that could make her find her way or bring back her footprints. She felt the valley expand inside her chest and throat, and could not contain the vacuum expanding inside her. She began to turn away from where she stood. But perhaps this great space was what the queen moth, the tortoise, the murmuration, had spoken about.

She let the space fill her wholly. "I see you," she said. "I see you in my throat. I see you in my chest. I can see this. I won't disappear this way."

Then the space stretching inside her began to evaporate like a mist, each moment thinner than before. Her mind was quiet. The valley before her was a valley; not inside her. What was inside her but a firmly beating heart—a heart either crushed or strained, but seen?

This is how a human being can change.
There is a worm
addicted to eating grape leaves.
Suddenly, he wakes up,
call it grace, whatever, something
wakes him, and he is no longer a worm.
He is the entire vineyard,
and the orchard too, the fruit, the trunks,
a growing wisdom and joy
that does not need to devour.

Rumi

The tulip bulb in Luna's knapsack began to peek out of the opening over time. The bulb's green finger reached out, and Luna knew it must be planted as soon as possible. Each new day it looked a little different than before. The red bud split open. It needed earth and water to continue living, but she couldn't plant it just anywhere: not too near other plants where it would be deprived of water, not where it would be eaten by an animal, or constricted by rocks. To let the moth's precious gift shrivel up on her back was her worst fear.

It seemed to become heavier with time and her back began to sting with the strain. She tried readjusting the sack, wearing the shoulder straps on one side or cradling it in her arms. Each new position ached after a while.

She continued heading west, though she hadn't seen the turrets of the castle in some time. Did that mean she was close or off course? The landscape had been mainly fir trees for some time, and they were beginning to grow sparse.

She arrived one morning at a grove of beech trees, illuminated in a verdant halo hiding the sun. In the midst of the trees stood a large stone manor.

Wildflowers grew among the beeches to one side of the manor, and extended out to a meadow farther than Luna could see. A mélange of bluebells, lupins, peonies, poppies, snapdragons, Queen Anne's lace, echinacea and many more types of flowers covered every inch of earth. A warmth kindled inside her chest, and she hardly felt the weight of her flower anymore. This … this was where she would plant her flower, under the beech trees, where flowers belonged. If only she could find a place where it would have enough room to grow. The flowers grew in such abundance that the ground could not be seen.

Just then a groundhog scuttled into sight from behind a wall of the manor. He was watering plants with a golden watering can, and wore a belt with gardening clippers, a hacksaw, and a flask of water attached. By all appearances, he was the gardener. Surely he wouldn't mind an extra flower being planted near the grounds.

"Excuse me," Luna addressed him. "I've been traveling for a long time and just found this grove. I was admiring your field of flowers. Do you think there's an empty space here where I could plant this tulip?" she asked, holding out the withering plant.

"Oh, why sure," he replied in an accent Luna couldn't place. "Any little plot with nothing growing is fine. Better get it in the earth with some water on those roots. The petals are looking a bit sad."

Luna scowled and hoisted the plant up her hip. She eyed the premises again. She couldn't choose a spot where it would clearly be out of place, but she also saw no room in the meadow where she could plant without unearthing other flowers.

She glanced at the limp petals of her tulip. They were indeed in need of water. "Any suggestions?" she asked, trying to hide her annoyance.

"There should be some little spot with some empty earth around here. Just be careful not to disturb any of the other plants." He continued watering plants along the perimeter of the wall, unconcerned.

Luna shifted the weight of the flower, unsure what to do next. Anger welled up in her throat. "I can't carry this much longer or it really *shall* die! It's heavy."

The groundhog paused, glancing sideways at her. "Well, leave it there, then. I can plant it somewhere when I'm done with my watering."

It was unthinkable. Just surrender it to someone else's care, drop it off as though it were a telegram? "No, I can't!" she protested. *Useless*, she thought, and trudged away in frustration.

"Pardon!" he called. "Go knock on that door," he said, gesturing to the stone house. "He owns the meadow and this land. He'll find a place."

"Who will?"

He looked at her strangely, a subtle lock of disbelief passed over his face. "The Bear," he replied.

She was stunned. "*The* Bear?"

"The only."

"But he lives in a castle."

He suppressed a chuckle. "This is a castle. Look up."

The trees' leaves grew so thick, their stature so tall, that they covered the greater portion of the wall face, hiding its great height.

She pulled the bell cord hanging in the threshold and heard a distant bong inside. Birds chattered in the trees, a slight breeze blew, but she heard no movement inside.

"May I help you?" a deep voice asked from behind her. She turned around and saw a great brown bear larger than life, compared to her, standing on all fours a stone's throw away. He tilted his head, his eyes searching. She nodded, unable to respond.

"What do you have there?" he asked.

"Sir, this…" she gestured toward the flower, then began again. "My name is Luna. I've come to see you from very far away."

"Thank you for coming, Luna. I would like to see you too. Your flower looks like it needs care, and you look as though you need rest."

She nodded.

"May I take it?" he asked.

"Thank you, sir. But I need to plant it somewhere safe." She clutched it closer.

The Bear walked toward the threshold in large, slow movements. "You're welcome to stay."

"Thank you, sir," she said.

"Come inside, have something to eat and drink. There's a place for your flower here. I can plant it where it will grow." He extended an open paw.

"Sir, I can't," she said with a wince. "This is the only thing I've carried with me. I can't part with it."

"I see. You don't have to let it go, then. Just let me hold it."

She felt the weight of it in her arms and wrists, and heaved a sigh. "All right. Hold it, please."

The Bear ushered her inside, taking the flower as though it were weightless. He showed her to a room with a four-poster bed, a fireplace and a window facing north. Luna hopped onto the windowsill and saw the sun setting to her left. The field of flowers below spread far beyond where the beech grove ended, out onto grassy hills in the distance.

"Could we put the flower in a pot where I can still see it?" she asked.

Bear agreed and came back with a terra-cotta pot full of soil and a watering can Luna's height. They planted it together, his giant paw placing it in, and her feet patting down the dirt. He poured water over the soil and waited for it to soak through. "I fear this beauty won't get the elements it needs indoors, not in this room. It would be such a shame to see it wilt when you've cared for it for so long," he said, placing it on the windowsill.

Luna glanced up at the window. *Imagine losing the gift only because I needed to keep it in sight,* she thought.

"You carried it quite far, didn't you?" he asked her. She nodded.

"I see. It may feel strange to see it anywhere besides your arms. But I'm glad you found me when you did. It was meant to be in one place."

"Yes, it was. A wonderful moth gave the bulb to me, and there just wasn't the right place to plant it until now." She hopped up onto the windowsill again and looked out at the field of flowers swaying in the breeze, which began to look like a gray sea in the evening haze. "Is there really a place for it here?" she asked.

"Yes. And for you too."

"Sir, I've waited so long to meet you. I can't express my gratitude to you for receiving me."

"Anyone who comes here is welcome. But I fear your tulip will struggle to survive indoors. I assure you it will bloom beautifully out in the field."

"Yes, you're right. But it feels strange to not keep it anymore." She felt sleep moving over her and excused herself to bed. Ah, a bed! How long it had been since she had lain on a bed. "Sir, do you really think it must be outside?" she asked as he started to leave.

He stopped. "There's so much for you to see here, Luna. Setting the flower in its place is only the first thing to do."

"Take it, then," she murmured, half asleep.

She opened her eyes some time later as moonlight drifted over her bed. Looking up at the windowsill, she saw that the tulip was gone. She felt a twinge inside her and her heartbeat quickened. She heaved a sigh and closed her eyes, part anxious and part relieved.

Luna had hoped the Bear would not ask her directly why she had come. As desperate as she had been to see him, she was fearful of how he would approach her disappearing.

He merely walked with her. He took her to the beech grove and the field of flowers, the fountains and

the stream, and one evening to the largest library she
had ever seen. Libraries she had browsed at Hickory's
or Chestnut's had consisted of five shelves or so. She
had borrowed every book, collected a sizable collec-
tion herself, and was always wanting to find more.

The walls of this library were bookshelves floor
to ceiling, as tall as trees, and built in winding undu-
lations around the room. Shadows from the blazing
fireplace danced across the floor and shelves. The
number of books was staggering, and Luna gazed
about her in awed silence.

"How does the world bear the weight of all this
knowledge?" she said to no one, hopping to the edge
of the room and pulling a book off the shelf, allowing
it to crack open in her hand. She scanned the pages
briefly before laying it on the floor and rummaging
through others. "I've searched for all of this." She
clutched at the cloth bindings on the shelves and
pulled out another whose title read, *Autonomy and
Synthesis*; the one to the side of it, *Ecologies of De-
ciduous Forests*. Both books tumbled to the ground,
and she leaned her nose against the row of books
on the shelf.

"It has to be here somewhere." she said, turning
to the Bear. "I've searched so long for all the secrets
that have been kept from me. They're hidden somewhere in all the dark places. They're in corners I

haven't found or pages I haven't read. I've longed for this room my whole life—every word ever written or spoken that I never found."

"I don't know what you want to find, or what purpose you want to fulfill when you find it," Bear said.

"Why have I always felt that there was more out there, far beyond my quaint cottage, my quaint woods, my short, quaint life? I need to find where dawn starts and somehow feel a part of the sun's rising. Then I could be at peace."

"How many of these books would help you reach that place?" he asked.

She scanned the room again, shaking her head. "It isn't an amount, but the *right* things. I knew in my heart all these things existed, but I didn't know what they were. I needed … something that would tell me how to be free."

"I fear it may take more than these books," he replied. He paused for a moment. "I noticed something."

She felt her heart beating faster, afraid he would confirm that she was indeed disappearing, and maybe that he could not help her.

"Many creatures I've met have a rapacious need to fix something. I can see it in your eyes now. But this isn't the real you. No one is rapacious at their core, only afraid."

"How could I not be afraid?" she blurted out.

Haven't you *seen* me?" she exclaimed, holding out her forearms.

"Yes, I have. I know. It's all right," he said. "You can stay here as long as you need. But what you want is not where you're looking, not in all this," he said, looking around the room.

"I need it to be here," she said. "Or somewhere. If it's not ... how can I be free?"

"I know you want to be free. But know that everyone else does too; and everyone is trying, in some way, whether they're disappearing or not."

You were inside my hand.
I kept reaching around for something.
I was inside your hand, but I kept asking questions
 of those who know very little.
I must have been incredibly simple or drunk or insane
to sneak into my own house and steal money, to climb
over the fence and take my own vegetables. But no more.
I've gotten free of that ignorant fist that was pinching
and twisting my secret self.
The universe and the light of the stars come through me.
I am the crescent moon put up over the gate to the festival.

Rumi

*L*una stayed, but she did not know how long. Time did not seem to be a quality that existed with the Bear, at least not the way it existed before; not in a way that felt as though something were draining away. Now the colors that gradated around her she regarded with a newfound wonder. That change should happen at all felt more like true life than she had felt before.

And was it possible that she was changing with it? She pondered for some time what she and the Bear had spoken of in the library. Could it be true that her estrangement made her closer to others than she had ever imagined? Was every creature merely striving to feel their weight, to matter at all? Were they all heaving each breath just to belong?

She went to the Bear one evening with a sense of resolve. She was ready, she told him, not to see what she had always seen, but to see what he saw. Perhaps her scope had been too myopic. Perhaps she had seen too little with her own eyes, and the partial truths had morphed into her erasure.

"Would you show me what you've been able to see all along?" she asked him. "You've been able to look out and see the land from all directions. Perhaps you could even see my part of the forest. Where is the highest place in the castle?"

"What you'll find may surprise you," he replied.

"Yes, of course. But nevertheless …" she trailed off. Her ears and whiskers fidgeted at the thought. "I need to see what you see. You have the highest view of anyone from up here. I bet you could see me as my steps were disappearing behind me, and you know everywhere I've been. Take me to the top, please. If I can find the end, maybe it won't matter that I have no history. I'll be home."

Bear acquiesced and led the way to one of the western towers as Luna followed behind. She felt as light as a feather, and it seemed the only part of her body that was left was her heart, beating like a drum.

He stopped in front of an arched wooden door and turned to her. "This western turret is the highest in the castle. But brace yourself." He opened the door and they ascended a spiral staircase behind it.

The sun had just set, and from the ground Luna could see only the pale blue sky over the battlements. She ran around the court in an aimless frenzy.

"I can't see over! Let me on your back!" she urged.

"Come," he said as he walked toward the edge. Luna scurried over to him and climbed up his hind leg onto his back. Clutching at his fur, infinity hit her.

An ocean like glass lay below them as far and wide as the eye could see. Hundreds of miniature islands dotted the ocean. They lay as far in every direction as she could see. On each island stood a castle. Some were only a short boat ride away, others so far they seemed more like a mirage. Each distant island appeared as though it were the farthest, yet looking beyond each one she could make out yet another island even farther in the distance. The staggering number continued across a seemingly endless horizon.

"Is this the top of the world?" she whispered in awe.

"In some way, yes. Tell me what you see."

"Castles … forever. I can hardly bear to look at it. It's too much to fathom. Are there other bears like you in all of them?" she asked wide-eyed.

"No, I am the only Bear. And this is my castle. These castles hold the histories of everyone who has lived."

"Everyone … ?" she murmured. One question hovered in the air, and she was afraid to ask it. She swallowed hard. "It's more than I could have imagined. It's too much to hold in my mind at once. How can

I ever make sense of infinity? I can't sort through it
or experience it. To even think of what all the castles
contain—you alone is enough to know in a lifetime! If
I began to long for it, I would be undone. There isn't
even enough *of* me to long for all of it."

"You've certainly tried," he said.

"Yes, it's as though my very organs know everything that isn't mine. And none of those castles are."
She turned toward him. "Why did you show me this?
You knew I would long for these things. Why would
you—" She stopped and hopped down to go back.

He took one step in her direction and scooped her
up in his paw. "Tell me," he admonished.

She paused and held his gaze for a moment.
"Where's my history," she said, though it was not a
question. "Where am *I*? My footprints won't even
stay in the ground. I'm disappearing! You show me all
there is to be desired and I'm not a part of it! I have
no castle. I'm no more than the air I'm breathing now,
and I'll be less than that soon enough. Just take me
away. I can't look anymore."

Luna lay prostrate in bed that evening. She felt
dizzy, and wanted sleep to come. Bear had taken her
to her room and laid her in bed. She lay motionless
with her face buried underneath her arms. Bear shuffled around and she soon heard cracklings of a fire in
the fireplace. She dozed off for a while and reawak-

ened. It was dark out by then.

Bear was dozing by the fireplace, breathing in long, dome-like breaths. Luna got out of bed and hopped onto the windowsill. Bear stirred at her movement and opened one eye. He joined her and rested his chin on the ledge. They looked out into the sky in silence for some time.

"That is the thing," Luna said distantly. "The thing that's always been kept from me. I just didn't imagine I'd feel even further away from it when I found it."

"What was kept from you?" he asked.

She thought for a moment. "I hardly know. It's as though there was a secret I didn't know. I couldn't ever see all of it. It was like trying to remember a whole dream long after it happened.

"Perhaps it's where I can feel that I'm inside my very own body, I can feel every part of it, and I can feel others feeling the same way. Where I'm here and I'm me, and you're here and you're you. And we can both feel each other feeling inside our own skin. And somehow you know you're not searching anymore because you're in the homest home you could ever want."

Bear's brown eyes met her gray eyes. His breath swayed her fur back and forth. "I think, you want to feel ... alive. And you want to feel *felt*."

"Yes, I *do*! But it isn't enough to just *feel* that way. In my forest I did so want to feel alive, but I also wanted to feel *part* of it. It isn't enough to feel alive if it's not part of a story. It isn't enough to feel anything if it doesn't all connect. Why on earth would I want one piece from a hundred different puzzles?"

"You told me you didn't have a history. But its depth depends on where you're willing to go," Bear said.

"I came here, didn't I? What else can I do?"

"Seek the truth, first. Never accept a lie—even if you're the liar."

"That's all I've ever searched for!" she protested.

"You've sought knowledge, among other things, yet you've wounded yourself with lies you've swallowed."

"I don't—lie," she began.

"Not even now?"

She avoided the gaze she felt boring into her.

"Why are your footprints disappearing?" he asked her.

"That's why I came to you. I thought you would tell me. But instead you showed me something that only makes this more painful."

"Luna, I'm here now," he said. His huge paw ran gently over her ears and back. "The truth takes courage. Tell me."

The only sound in the room came from the flames in the fireplace, like deep breathing, waiting for her reply.

"If I only ever see one set of tracks, mine don't matter. I don't feel real at all."

He stroked her ears with exquisite softness. "You've gone further tonight than you did in coming here."

"I've gone further than I ever thought I could," she said, burying her face in her hands. "But it all feels like one big nothing. My feet have been worn down with wandering—I felt like a speechless animal out there—and still I can't make my days mean anything."

"Did you ever think that whoever looks out from their turret is also looking back at you? When you saw that horizon, did you imagine that others look out and see what you saw? Everyone looks out and sees the same thing. But none of them know the corridors or rooms of this castle, or know your history, the one you say you don't have."

She sighed heavily. "I suppose they do see the same thing. So why is there so much distance between all of us? I don't want to be a secret all my life. I want to be known. If we all know we're apart, why can't we find each other?"

"We're trying," he replied.

Luna nodded. "Bear, is there any way to go to the other castles? I came to yours. Couldn't we go elsewhere? I want to see them too."

"Certainly. You could. I think you've been trying for longer than you know."

She furrowed her eyebrows, confused.

"You could spend the rest of your life rowing to each one, going to the top, and seeing more. And still your own footprints would not stay where you put them, and you would not be in your own castle."

Luna felt as though the air had been taken out of her throat. Every so often, perhaps only a few times, a shift may take place inside a creature's body that leaves the mind clear and empty and spacious. It has no use for thoughts. One hears one's breath, that is all. The mind is open like a cup; it is being filled, and yet, it is not full. This was the shift that Luna felt. She closed her eyes in bed that night and listened to her heartbeat. How much she had sought to fill the finite spaces inside, how much hunger had driven her. Now her chest felt like the whole universe; not as it had in her forest, as a black hole—simply being; a great expanse, without ambition, without lack.

Last night as I was sleeping
I dreamt—marvelous error!—
that I had a beehive
here inside my heart.
And the golden bees
were making white combs
and sweet honey
from my old failures.

Antonio Machado

One afternoon, Luna and Bear were ambling around the grounds in the beech grove. Luna's mind had been blissfully empty as she collected wildflowers and lay on the grass.

By and by, she spotted another rabbit across the meadow who looked remarkably familiar, just like Luna herself. The newcomer stood on her hind legs with her forearms in the air near her cheeks, as if peering through a knothole. She beat the air, as though there were a wall in front of her. She changed her posture between standing up and resting on all fours.

Luna watched her, puzzled. There was something familiar about her. And why did it seem as though she were unable to come any closer?

"Bear, do you see that rabbit over there?" she asked. "What is she doing? Why does she seem—trapped?"

"She's stuck behind a glass wall."

"A glass wall? Here? How is that possible?"

"Well, there isn't a wall here, is there?"

"Of course not. Why is she doing that?"

"She thinks there's a wall there, so she cannot go any farther."

Luna skittered toward her. Could this rabbit see her, she wondered. Could she speak to her? She stopped a couple yards away to observe. The rabbit stood on her hind legs with her forefeet seemingly pressed against a vertical surface, sniffing the air. Luna hopped across the invisible barrier and back several yards down from the other rabbit. She could pass freely, so surely this was an illusion.

"Come pass over!" she called. The rabbit looked longingly at her, though she did not seem to hear. Luna stood in front of her, edging her hand across the barrier. The rabbit watched in wonder at Luna's hand.

"Can't you see? I'm right here. You can touch me. Just step over." Again the rabbit put her forefeet in the air, as though leaning against glass, and shook her head.

"You seem so familiar," Luna murmured. "Give me your hand." She reached hers up toward the rabbit's in midair, and placed her palm against the stranger's. "I can see you," she said, looking into her eyes. "Don't try to push against it anymore."

The stranger descended back onto all fours,

turned, and scampered away.

"Wait!" Luna called after her. "We're right here! You can come too!"

But the rabbit continued deeper into the forest. Luna's heart sank. Running back to Bear, she asked. "Will she come? What's wrong? Is she really stuck on the other side?"

Bear looked distantly after the other rabbit. "Yes. Some creatures have not arrived yet. It's a long way from where they came; their trek is so long they sometimes think they could never not be lost."

Luna felt her chest tighten. "Bear … did you ever see me before, around here?"

He cast a sideways glance at her with a smile at the corner of his mouth, then picked her up gingerly in his paws. "I've always seen you. All creatures get stuck behind walls only they can see. Sometimes the walls disappear, but then there are more."

"Do some of them get stuck forever?" Luna asked.

"Well, yes, truthfully."

Luna exhaled heavily. "I can't imagine wandering in the forest forever.

"Well, think of it like this. From your perspective they're stuck out there. But what about you? What might you look like to someone who's beyond you? Perhaps there are other places you haven't allowed yourself to go where others are already. To see the wall you are behind, that is the first step. But how wonderful that you're here!"

Upon returning to her room, Luna placed a crown of clovers she had made on the bureau near the window. She turned to Bear who was with her. "Whatever happened to my flower?" she inquired, somewhat anxious about where it was now living.

"It's with the others in the field. I transplanted it into the ground myself the day you arrived at my door."

"With the others? I didn't want it there. I don't know where it is now. It doesn't mean anything in the field. It all looks like one big sea of pink and white from here. Why did you plant mine where it can't be seen?"

"Because you belong here, too. I plant all the flowers entrusted to me. They all need to be planted, including yours. Just look," he said, gesturing toward the window. Luna hopped up onto the windowsill and looked below.

"Each of them was once a bulb traveling somewhere else, as yours once was. Each one set theirs down here, and became part of the field. They wouldn't have come if they hadn't needed to, in their own ways. Your journey makes up part of this field too."

One afternoon, Luna was walking in the brook
near the grounds, collecting rocks from the brook
bed in a basket. Some smooth, flat stones she used to
practice skipping. The more interesting ones required
closer examination. The clear surface of the brook
sparkled in the sun, making even ordinary rocks ap-
pear more beautiful.

One particularly bright reflection made her
squint. One was very unlike the others. She jostled
it around gently with her toes, wondering if it were
a mirage. Bracing the stone with her toe, she bent
to pluck it up. Dripping wet, a plum-size sapphire
gemstone of a deep greenish-blue sparkled in the
sunlight. She gazed into it, marveling at the colors
shifting as she rocked it back and forth. The facets
glimmered from deep blue to emerald, cyan, aqua, and
topaz. The translucent blue gave it an appearance of
aqueous purity. Its splendid beauty left her breathless.
For a moment, she wanted to swallow it, to keep it
safe, with her.

"Luna!" she heard Bear call. He saw her from afar
and waved. Startled, she held the gem to her chest. He
ambled over to her with a curious expression. "How
have you been getting on?" he asked.

She nodded.

"Have you found anything interesting today?"

She swallowed, afraid she had found something

perhaps too precious. What would he say if he saw it?

"What have you got there?" he asked, looking at her hand clutched to her chest.

"This was in the brook," she replied, drawing her hand down to reveal part of the gem.

Bear glanced at the gemstone in her palm, then back at her. "I see," he said. "What a precious stone you've found."

It caught the sunlight in a nearly blinding way in her palm. "This," she said, looking at the gem. "This is what I want. I must keep this with me."

"It is a rare beauty indeed. But it is not something to be hoarded," said Bear.

Luna was taken aback at Bear's response. She closed her hand around the stone and took a step away from him.

"It is not a thing to be possessed. You can attempt to hoard it but you can't swallow it as you desire. It will always be outside of you."

Luna's jaw fell at Bear's telepathic remark. "I *will* have it! This is what I've longed for! This gem is more beautiful than anything I've ever seen," she said, gazing at it with tenderness and wonder. "Everything I thought I wanted was only to possess something of such purity and beauty."

Just then the stone slipped slowly through her hand. She grasped at it with her other hand, but it fell through nonetheless. Frantically she tried to pick it up, but to no avail. "Oh, please! Please help me pick it up!" she pleaded with Bear.

"It isn't a thing you can possess," he replied. "You cannot be satisfied if you resolve that it's outside of you."

"You don't understand!" she wailed. Her fur bristled in panic. "I must have this! This is what I've wanted all along. I don't want anything but this precious jewel! I don't care about the castles or your libraries or any of that. I just want this to call my own!" Again she splashed her forefeet in the water trying to grab it, but it evaded her. "If you don't give me this gem I'll never forgive you!" she cried.

"Listen, I am incapable of giving it to you. You can't possess it."

She looked at the brook, defeated. "I'm nothing without this," she murmured. Impulsively she grabbed at the stone and flung her arm to throw it. Yet it lay still with the other rocks, and she leapt away in chagrin. She bounded toward the forest in no particular direction, then collapsed at the base of a tree. Time passed and the sun began to descend.

Why had she come to the castle when she could never find what she had been seeking? Thinking of the gem's rare beauty, she could feel its weight in her palm. Was holding it as close to it as she would ever get? All the beauty, that is what she had wanted for so long, inside her, before she had found the Bear. The avarice for an essence she could never see or touch had consumed her. How unworthy of the stone she felt now. If she could not possess it or even hold it, would she run forever, weary and entangled in cupidity?

She fell asleep as the forest grew dark and awoke to a rustling noise, feeling heavy and disoriented. The faintest hue of blue seeped through the treetops.

"There you are," Bear's resonant voice spoke. "When you didn't come back, I got up early to come look for you. Sunrise will be here soon. I wanted to show you something."

"I don't think I want to," she muttered.

"Please come back," he said, extending his paw toward her. "I can show you what you truly want. Behind what you may think you want lies your true desire. The jewel is a good thing indeed. But if you only knew your desire is so much deeper than that."

Wearily, she crawled into his paw, expecting nothing. Her eyes were heavy, and she planned to sleep before leaving for good.

Holding her in one arm, Bear carried her back to the castle. It was nearly dawn when he climbed the steps to the eastern tower.

"Please, not the castles," she pleaded, half asleep.

"I'm taking you to the eastern tower. The sun

will be above the horizon soon, and you will see everything."

The horizon lightened to gold, and the ashy blue of the sky began to burn away into fires of pink, peach, and orange. The sky blazed with gold as the sun rose. Silhouettes of trees and mountains colored into branches and valleys.

As the sun rose fully above the horizon, it softened from a disk of fire and expanded into a formless glow. The horizon and all the world below faded until all that could be seen was an empyreal glow that swept Luna up, pulling her toward its center. A golden circle embraced her. There were no more pieces, only a great oneness that encompassed her. "Where am I? And who are you?" she implored.

Like a mountain, telling its story in silent equanimity, a voice answered her. "I am your Mother, your great origin. I am the arms that hold you. I am the home you long for, the love that fills you. I am One, and you are all of you in me."

"How long I've wanted you—since I was born—and I didn't know you! This is everything!"

"Yes, everything! I have gathered to me all the pieces that were scattered. You have not been lost or wasted or unseen. I have known you and brought you to my heart. All of you is here."

Basking in this infinite center, Luna knew these

words to be true. "I belong here. I am whole."

After the glow dissipated, Bear instructed Luna to go back into the forest and wait. He could not say what for, but that there was something else to come.

Deep in the woods, she waited. For an invitation? A message? Would the golden circle embrace her again, and this time whisk her away forever?

At once a stag with green fur and antlers leapt out of the woods and stopped in front of her. Flowered vines coiled around its body. It looked boldly into her eyes before kneeling its head to the ground. Surely this creature had come to take her away. Luna climbed up onto the base of its antlers. It bounded deeper into the forest in giant leaps, descending like a feather falling on the ground.

Finally it slowed its stride, its chest heaving in and out. They had come to a tiny verdant clearing. Before them lay a giant green nest underneath a dogwood tree. Fixated, Luna climbed to the ground and up into the nest. She had been brought here for a purpose, there was no question. She sat in the nest with a patient knowing. "Mother," she prayed, "I began somewhere. Where did I go all this time? Show me where I am now."

A white blossom fell from the tree and whirled toward the ground. It grew as it fell, spinning slowly as the petals spun around like ribbons around a maypole. A woman emerged from the blossom and placed her feet on the ground. She wore a robe of translucent silk, and her white hair gathered around her knees. She was not old, though her blue eyes held the fullness of knowledge. Neither was she young, though her countenance held the peace and joy of one's first spring before winter. She smiled at Luna. "You are in the right place," she said.

Surely this woman is the form of the golden circle, Luna thought.

"You've told me what you desire," the woman said. "I loved you at the castles, in the dark, in the wilderness, in your forest, in your beginning. And I love you now. I called you here. I want you to see the truth."

"Mother …" Luna sighed, and climbed out of the nest. "If I have not been lost, where did all my footprints go?"

The woman paused, looking into Luna's eyes. "Luna, love even this … you gave them away with every step you did not claim. You covet the happiness of others, the ease of others, the castles of others. See how the fire of your passion was you trying to love yourself. Do not hate her. See how she still wants the best for you." And she placed her hand on Luna's heart.

Luna felt her chest heat as the warmth from the woman's palm emanated into her.

"Your envy is a heart longing to bloom into all it values and desires to be," the woman said. "If you only knew your true goodness. Underneath all your wanting, beyond the small self you may reject, still inside is your goodness. Do not hate your small self, she wants so to be happy. We all want that."

She reached into her robe and pulled out the sapphire stone from the brook. "I believe you desired to have this," she said, holding it out in her pale palm.

Luna's stomach turned upside down at seeing the iridescent gleam, seeming more brilliant than ever.

"This stone is too small for you. If you were to have this, all you could do is hold it in your hand and admire it in longing."

"Oh, but I would love that!" Luna assured her.

The woman looked into her eyes. "How would you like to *be* this stone?"

Luna's eyes widened. Her curiosity was more than she could bear. She nodded, not sure if anything had come out of her mouth.

"To me, this is merely a stone," the woman said, holding it up between her thumb and forefinger. "When I see you, I see thousands of stones. I see ten thousand facets of sapphire shining in the sun."

"What do you mean?" Luna asked, astounded.

The woman smiled. "Yes. Come see your reflection." She beckoned Luna out of the clearing and into the trees. They walked a short distance until they came to a small, clear pond.

Peering into the water, Luna saw that her face was made entirely of sapphires. Gaping, she touched the deep teal and cyan of her face, only to notice that her hands were also made of the same gem. She stepped away from the water and looked at herself. Her whole body was indeed that of the stone. Speechless, she gazed into the woman's blue eyes in a trance. "How?" she whispered.

The woman's nose crinkled up in a delighted smile. "You can finally see things as they are!"

"How can I ever repay you?"

"Child, I have not done anything! I did not turn you into these gems. You're seeing what's really here."

"But I've never been this beautiful in my life!" she exclaimed. "How can you say I've been this way all along?"

"What would you say if I agreed with you? Are you looking for confirmation that your deepest fears are true?"

"Oh no! That would be my worst nightmare. My reflection before this seemed so obviously unremarkable. When I spoke of it, I guess I wanted confirmation that it *wasn't* true."

"All these fears have been as real as these gems are now. But not true."

"They're not true anymore. I know. I'm finally the good I wanted to be," Luna said, marveling at her jeweled arms she held in front of her.

"Oh, Luna," the woman said, stooping to put her hand on Luna's shoulder, "You were always the good you wanted to be. Behind your fear is the real you, the free you.

The woman reminded her that the gemstones would fade from visibility, but not from existence. "You need not chase this anymore," she told her. "You have seen your essential nature. As you walk your way on this earth, forgive your shame as a fearful heart seeking to preserve itself. Forgive your longing as your heart's deepest desire for goodness. Redeem them. Your nature is still there, that is what lives beyond all our days, beyond our striving.

"Come, I will take you home." She took Luna's hand in hers, and they ascended off the ground. The woman looked down at Luna and smiled. "Don't be afraid!"

As they rose higher, the woman placed Luna on her shoulders and drew her attention to the field of flowers that blanketed the ground farther than they could see. "There's the flower you carried with you!" the woman proclaimed, pointing down. "It's bloomed so beautifully!"

How funny, Luna thought. *What was she*

*talking about? How on earth could she find my flower
in that sea?*

They flew down and landed gently in the field.
"See? It's here," the woman said, stroking the stem of a
beautiful red tulip.

"That *is* my flower," Luna remarked in awe. "How
on earth did you make it out in all of this?"

"When you've known each one as long as I have
…" the woman chuckled, sinking her toes into the soil.

"Oh," Luna exhaled. "When Bear took it, I was sad
that I wouldn't see it anymore." She felt a twinge in
her stomach. "I guess it seemed lost."

"Lost? Why, this is the only place it truly belongs!
It's here with all the others, where it was always meant
to be. It's a singular beauty, and yet contributes to the
whole field. It has thrived in the soil among the thousands of others that took their journeys here. Trust
me, you were always meant to be here."

A chuckle escaped Luna's throat, turning into a
laugh. She sighed and collapsed on the ground, looking up at the evening sky.

That night, they floated in through Luna's
bedroom window and the woman placed her
on the ground.

Luna searched for words to part by, but what
words could express what should be said? "I …," Luna
paused and sighed.

The woman's face cracked into a smile. "I know," she whispered. "It's time to sleep." Her hair lit up in a glow, traveling throughout her body. "I am always here, your center." Her glowing light faded and a white dogwood blossom fell where she had stood.

Luna plucked the blossom from the floor and kissed it. "Thank you," she whispered.

LUNA DIDN'T TELL BEAR that she would leave. He seemed to know that she was ready.

"Go back to the lake where you arrived. This will help you," he said, handing her a map with the route marked. "When you arrive back at the lake, go for a swim. You needn't worry about how to get back home after that."

Luna headed east late the next morning while Bear watched her leave. After she had gone a short distance she heard him call her name. She stopped and turned around.

"I could follow you home!" he called with a smile.

For a moment she wasn't sure what he meant. He laughed, and she looked around. Then she noticed it. Faintly, but consistently, the path she had just trod led all the way from Bear to where she stood. Even in the grass, she could see the path her feet had made.

She stood for a moment looking from Bear to her

path to her feet. Her eyes moistened. "Thank you!" she called. It didn't seem to be exactly fitting, but it was all that came to her.

She counted the days of her journey this time, ticking them off on the map with a charcoal pencil Bear had given her. At night she studied the map, trying to make out the route she had originally taken. She could see that she had sidled too far south and had then traveled far around the castle in a northerly direction before finally coming upon it that auspicious day. How much extra time she had spent without a map to guide her. Her journey back to the lake was not a short one, though it felt altogether more purposeful than the first. Time did not blend and muddle into itself as it had before.

The lake waited for her return. It was still, a sheet of forest-green glass from end to end. She walked down to the shore and took off the drawstring knapsack the queen moth had given her with the map inside. She drank from a shallow edge and then gazed across the lake. In the silence and stillness, a figure across the water walked slowly down to drink. Four spindly legs moved in slow motion, and a graceful neck bent toward the water. Luna felt a twinge in her chest, watching this peaceful creature who had blessed her with the beauty of possibility so long ago.

The deer looked up in Luna's direction. Luna

could not tell if Tamsen could see her tiny body from across the lake, but she raised her arm and waved. Running away from the shore, she climbed up a tree as far as she could go. Tamsen raised her head high. Luna smiled. If Tamsen could speak to the trees, surely she could hear the words Luna didn't speak just then. *I don't need to be understood. But I know you understand.*

Tamsen stamped her hoof on the ground, then turned to go. She turned her head back in Luna's direction before disappearing into the trees.

Luna waded into the water and swam several strokes as Bear had instructed her. She floated on her back, looking at the pale sky. The sun had nearly set.

Wondering what would happen, how she might get home from there, she took a gulp of air and dove under, paddling her way down. She came up gasping for air and wiped the water from her eyes. Upon opening her eyes, she stopped. Cottonwood trees stood along the water's edge. She was not in the lake at all. Here she was in the pond near her home.

We shall not cease from exploration
And the end of all our exploring
Will be to arrive where we started
And know the place for the first time.

T.S. Eliot

*L*una decided it was time for a new roof. The season was some time between spring and summer; not yet to the solstice, but some ambrosial midseason, warm with a cool breeze, that made one walk with a quicker step. A fresh thatch was the renovation the house needed in that weather.

Luna was in the process of installing short wooden posts between the frame of the roof and the top of the walls to allow for a fresh breeze to come through, when a familiar striped creature strolled by.

"Hello!" Chestnut called to her.

Luna tried to wave and say hello while clutching a hammer and post, with a nail between her lips.

"Why does it seem like an eternity since we saw each other?" Chestnut asked, leaning against the picket fence.

Luna chuckled and dropped the nail. Setting aside the hammer and post at the top of the wall, she climbed down the ladder. She leapt toward

Chestnut and kissed her on the cheek. "It has been!" she exclaimed.

Chestnut beamed. "Take a break, would you? Hickory's coming to my place with some fish he caught this afternoon. I'm making a pie. Come on over when you get cleaned up," she said. "It's looking wonderful!" she added as she turned and waddled off.

Luna washed, then prepared muffins for the evening. With the muffins tied in a cloth, she put on her shoes and grabbed a light coat. A breeze blew the tall grasses on either side of the dirt road, making them sway like waves. Their billows seemed to buttress her like hands.

Mother, I'm here. I'm here. I'm here. Help me feel that.

A strange gift, to be able to create one's future, one's present, from scratch. It is a freedom given to those who were born and lived. That each breath one took, each step one placed on the ground, one might create their story of belonging, or mattering at all. Never was a gift so precious, so terrible.

A flock of birds flew overhead, and Luna watched them dip and sway. She heard the whoosh of air as they dove down then swooped up before flying away. Her breath caught in her throat and she gaped up in wonder.

"Luna!" a familiar voice called as she neared

Chestnut's home. Hickory had seen her coming and he waved and scurried toward her. "You're here!" he exclaimed as he embraced her.

"Yes, I'm here," she replied with a smile she couldn't suppress.

"Come inside!" Chestnut beckoned to them from inside. "And would you take off your shoes? I don't want any dirt tracked in."

Luna slipped off her shoes before she crossed the threshold, and glanced back at the path. So many tracks had been made, one creature's across another's, that they were indistinguishable from one another. Hers were there somewhere among them, till the next rainfall. She wiped her feet on the mat and closed the door.

The End

Bibliography

p. 6   Rilke, Rainer Maria. "I Am Praying Again, Awesome One." Rainer's Book of Hours: Love Poems to God, translated by Anita Barrows and Joana Macy, Riverhead Books, 1996, pp. 97-98.

p. 65   Serrat, Joan Manuel. Lyrics to "Cantares." Performed by Joan Manuel Serrat, Novola, 1969. https://genius.com/Joan-manuel-serrat-cantares-lyrics.

p. 75   Rumi. "The Worm's Waking." The Essential Rumi, translated by Coleman Barks, Harper Collins, 1995, pp. 265.

p. 86   Rumi. "Wax." The Essential Rumi, translated by Coleman Barks, Harper Collins, 1995, pp. 138.

p. 95   Machado, Antonio. "Last Night As I Was Sleeping." Times Alone Selected Poems of Antonio Machado, translated by Robert Bly, Wesleyan University Press, 1983, pp. 43.

p. 114   Eliot, T.S. "Little Gidding." T.S. Eliot: The Complete Poems and Plays, Harcourt, Brace, & World, Inc., 1971, pp. 145.

About the Author

Julianne Bigler has been plumbing the depths of the human experience and the psyche in her schooling, personal life, and through this story. Her body of writing spans a personal blog, poetry, content writing, and magazine journalism. She lives in San Diego. This is her first book.

About the Illustrator

Charles Lister is an illustrator who creates visual storytelling and conceptual ideation for games, film and books. He is currently working on his own story, *The Aegolist*, which has been a ten-year, evolving personal project, and a major source of inspiration behind his style. He lives in Santa Ynez, but specifically lives in the clouds.

www.ingramcontent.com/pod-product-compliance
Lightning Source LLC
Chambersburg PA
CBHW031345060726
47590CB00007B/2631